MW00939691

Picture Imperfect

By Mary Frame

Copyright © 2018 by Mary Frame
Cover design by James at Go On Write
www.goonwrite.com
Editing by Elizabeth Nover at Razor Sharp Editing
www.razorsharpediting.com

Any errors contained herein are likely the result of the author
continuing to change the manuscript after the line edits were
completed. I have problems. Don't judge me.

This book is a work of fiction. The names, characters, places, and
incidents are products of the writer's imagination, have been used
fictitiously, and are not to be construed as real. Any resemblance to
persons living or dead, actual events, locales, or organizations is
entirely coincidental.
All rights are reserved. No part of this book may be used or
reproduced in any manner without written permission from the
author.

*This book is dedicated
to everyone
who has ever felt
less than beautiful.*

Chapter One

A photograph is a secret about a secret. The more it tells you, the less you know.
            –Diane Arbus

Gwen

The day takes a sharp turn when my first client won't stop crying and then poops all over my new drop cloth.

Granted, he's only eight months old.

Even with the tears and turds, he's easier to deal with than his Upper East Side mother, who's decked out in clothing that costs more than my yearly income. She won't stop glaring at me as if the crying and subsequent diaper malfunction are somehow my fault.

The day gets moderately better when I get a call from a celeb rag that I've done work for previously.

"We've got a dinner at Miguel's that needs coverage."

"Celebrities pretending they don't want to be seen?"

"Pretty much. A group of new-money reality stars meeting for dinner to discuss some potential movie or TV show or who's the richest dumbass on the block—who knows. Liz is covering the article. She's expecting you at eight."

Eight. I was up preparing for my morning shoot at five.

I'm getting too old for this crap.

Over a year ago, after one of my shots landed on a billboard in Times Square, I thought my life would turn into a never-ending circle of money and fame and recognition. I was sure that one picture was my ticket to what I really wanted to do — serious shoots with serious people, traveling the world, and making a difference.

Instead, I'm schlepping my way through New York City every day and night, taking any job I can, trying to get a shot with a serious periodical, and praying for . . . something. Anything.

It's partially my fault. From the get-go I've been locked into the label of "former model Gwen." Not photographer Gwen who's been working her ass off for the last year. No one will take me seriously. And then when my personal life went sideways, I let it affect my professional life, which served to confirm the general opinion about former models attempting to break the mold. How can I prove myself when people refuse to look further than the surface?

I'm feeling every minute of my nearly twenty-eight years on this planet when I walk to Miguel's a few minutes before the scheduled time. I probably have another half hour before anyone arrives because it wouldn't be cool to show up — gasp — *on time*, like you don't have anything better to do. The truth is I really don't have anything better to do and I've given up pretending.

I talk to the hostess and then the manager about the party and they show me the area they're planning on setting everyone up in. It's not a huge guest list, about twelve.

The party room is through a large open doorway from the main restaurant space. Not exactly secluded, but I guess that's the point.

While I wait, I get an idea for the space and the lighting. The room is narrow and the furniture is dark. On top of that, it's all dim wall sconces that totally suck for getting detailed shots, so I ask to move a few lamps to make my job easier.

Thirty minutes later, people start showing up. The girls are mostly blonde, mostly Botoxed with unnaturally large lips and way too much makeup. The reporter covering the event is Liz Masterson. I've worked with her before on a few pieces. After quick greetings, she gives me the basics of the article — it's a short piece about a new reality show set in New York airing next season, some type of *Real World* thing but with trust-fund kids who are famous for being wealthy and not much else. She wants some simple, candid shots.

Once that's settled, I do my best to blend into the background, unnoticed.

It doesn't work.

A few of the girls keep thrusting out their chests and staring at the camera when they're supposed to be ignoring me. Does no one understand the meaning of the word candid? It's bad enough trying to catch decent shots when people look more plastic than real. Not that I'm judging. Do what makes you feel good about yourself, but they would be just as beautiful, if not more so, without the obviously added enhancements.

I get a few decent shots and then my camera lens wanders because I'm bored.

The viewfinder passes over a couple at a small table in the main room who are trying to look like they aren't fighting, but it's clearer than the most high-definition image ever recorded. They aren't speaking. Her mouth is tense, his jaw is tight.

Next to them, in a booth, a group of women are talking excitedly and laughing. Catching people in the act of true mirth is one of my favorite shots. It's completely unrestrained and honest, and while most people don't find it exactly flattering, I find it fascinating.

There's a sharp tug somewhere in the vicinity of my chest as I watch them. They remind me of my sisters, the only people I've ever been comfortable with without it turning around and biting me in the ass. I haven't talked and laughed with another woman without feeling anxious in, well, over a year.

Ugh, I'm so fucking depressing.

Moving on. I pan the camera over to the bar. Aha, a first date. I'd bet my Canon on it. She's sitting high and anxious in her seat and he's leaning back, all confident swagger and condescending smirk.

She gets up and heads toward the bathrooms, her fifties-style dark green A-line dress swinging as she walks, and he watches her disappear before pulling something out of his pocket and dumping it in her drink.

I snap the shutter a few times. "You dick," I mutter under my breath, already weaving through the tables.

My first reaction is to walk over and punch him in the throat the way my police officer sister Gemma taught me, but that would likely result in a lawsuit and/or getting thrown in jail for assault. Therefore, probably a bad idea.

Instead, I follow his victim to the bathroom.

I find her leaning over the sink, applying bright red lipstick. Thankfully, the bathroom is empty except for the two of us.

"Hey." I stop near the door, letting it shut behind me.

She blinks at me in the mirror and then turns. Only the top of her lip is red.

I pause for a second, unsure how to begin. "So, there's no easy way to say this, but your date put something in your drink. I have, um, a picture." I walk to the sink next to her and turn the camera in her direction, paging back to the photos I caught so she can see. "He moved pretty fast, but I got a good one of him putting whatever it was back in his pocket. Some kind of vial."

Her partially done-up mouth forms an O of surprise. "Oh, my God." One hand flutters to her chest. She's not from around here. If the Southern drawl didn't give her away, her innocent expression would have done so all on its own.

"How well do you know him?"

She shakes her head, her gaze moving from my face to the camera between us. "I don't. We just met. It's a blind date. This has never happened to me before. I didn't think . . . well." She straightens and puts a hand on her hip. "Now you know something like this did happen to one of my sorority sisters, back in Blue Falls, Texas. We were going to a frat party and she was assigned as the sober monitor, you know, to drive if needed and take care of the girls, and one of the guys tried to get her drunk but we could never figure out who it was. I wasn't there that night but I heard all about it and they never did figure out which of the guys spiked her drinks."

She stops suddenly, a red blush creeping up her cheeks, and she covers it with her hands.

"I'm so sorry I'm rambling on, I do that when I'm nervous. What do I do? Is there a back exit?" She peers behind me at the door.

"I think there is, but this guy will probably do the same thing again to someone else. Do you want to run, or do you want to help me nail him to the wall?"

Her eyes meet mine, wide and dumbfounded. Then she straightens, her mouth firming before she meets my eyes. "I ain't running anywhere. Let's get out the nails."

"Good. Can you go back and act normal? And this goes without saying, but don't drink your wine."

She nods. "I can do that. What are you going to do?"

"*We* are going to take this guy down. What's your name?"

"Scarlett Marie Jackson."

I nod. "Of course it is."

Five minutes later, she's taken a few deep breaths and finished applying her lipstick, and we've come up with a quick game plan. Once she gets over the shock, she is surprisingly assertive.

I find the manager and tell them what I saw, showing them the pictures I snapped of asshole Jerry drugging his date as proof, and they call the cops. The manager has a printer in his office and I have all my cables in my camera bag, so we're able to print off the money shot. There's no way I would ever hand my whole camera over to the cops. My Canon is like my right arm.

Once I get back to the dinner party, Liz is looking for me.

"What's going on?" She pulls me off to the side of the small room.

In a low voice, I quickly explain the situation. "I'm sorry, Liz. I have plenty of shots for your article, and I'll get more if you need them."

She waves me off. "That's fine. I can't believe that guy. Then again, maybe I can. Something similar happened to me in college." She shakes her head. "Don't we all have one of those stories?"

"Feels like it," I murmur.

"Anyway, good on you for stepping up and doing something."

"How could I not?"

One of the pouty blondes comes up and asks Liz a question and I resume my post, snapping pictures of celebs while keeping my side-eye out for Scarlett and her turd nugget of a date.

It takes nearly thirty minutes for the cops to arrive, and Scarlett does a surprisingly decent job of acting cool while not drinking her wine, although asshole Jerry keeps raising his glass in a toast to encourage her to take a sip. The bartender brings her a glass of water though, and she uses that as her excuse to leave off the wine for a bit.

When New York's finest finally arrive, management directs them to asshole Jerry.

The whole thing is surprisingly anticlimactic. I don't know what I expected, the guy to turn into OJ and jump into a white Bronco or something? But he doesn't even fight it.

When they say, "Come with us," he goes. He doesn't even seem surprised.

Dick.

I suppose it's lucky there isn't much of a kerfuffle, and the cops are in and out without any problems. I do snap a few pictures of them taking him away, because I have to. The look on his face is sinister in its complacency. Like he knew. Like he expected it.

My apartment is close enough to walk and I set a brisk pace home, hugging my sweater around me. Autumn is creeping into winter and the chill in the air portends the change of season. I can't wait to put on sweats and a lumpy T-shirt. The party scene is not for me. Not anymore.

It's dark outside, but there's plenty of illumination from the storefronts and streetlights. The errant cab passes by and a few people are walking the streets still. I lift my gaze to the black sky above.

No stars.

There never is with the ever-present light pollution and haze in the city. I miss sitting on the patio back home and counting the pinpricks above me.

"Wait!" A high-pitched voice calls out behind me before I wade too much into homesickness and general misery.

Scarlett is running after me, heels clattering on the pavement, dark hair flying behind her. She stops beside me. "I didn't get a chance to thank you properly."

"There's no need." I wave her off and keep walking.

She keeps pace beside me. "Are you kidding? If it wasn't for your help back there, well, I don't know what would have happened to me. Really." She shudders, then puts a hand on my arm. "You have to let me make it up to you somehow. Do you like cupcakes?"

"Cupcakes?"

"You know, little cakes with frosting."

"I know what cupcakes are." I'm just surprised she's offering. It's been so long since anyone has wanted to hang out with me or do anything for me, I've forgotten how to respond.

"I could make you some. Cooking and baking are my only real talents. It's why I'm here in New York, actually."

I stop walking and face her. "Your name is Scarlett, you're from Texas, and you make cupcakes? Are you for real?"

"Well it's like my granny always told me, reality is as real as beer and Skittles."

A startled laugh escapes me. "That doesn't even make sense."

"I never thought it did either, but then she always mixed up her phrases. So, cupcakes?" Scarlett's tone is hopeful. "Are you free tomorrow night?"

"I'm not sure, I might have another shoot. Sometimes they come up unexpectedly." It's true, but inside I know it's also an excuse, a defense mechanism.

"Too busy, huh? You sound an awful lot like the last three guys I dated." She sighs. "That's too bad. I don't know anyone in the city. I met Jerry on Grindr, have you ever been on there? Probably not, you're way too gorgeous to need help from some app where you have to swipe up and down and right and left and people just want to get laid. Anyway, I'm rambling again." The smile she gives me is apologetic. "You have to let me do something for you. You won't have to do anything or go anywhere. I can save you time so you can get to work. I'll bring you some of my famous red velvet cupcakes, everyone loves them, and even if you don't have time for a social life, you have to eat, don't you?"

"Yeah, sure," I agree. "So this is my stop. It was nice to meet you. Good luck with . . . everything." I wave and make an escape.

"Bye! Thank you again! Wait, I never got your—"

Her last word is cut off as I enter the building and shut the door behind me.

I never gave her my name.

Probably for the best.

~*~

9

My alarm goes off the next morning at seven. Bleary-eyed, I slam it into silence and then stumble out of bed. I didn't get to sleep until after midnight. Once I got home, I was a little amped up from the excitement of the night.

There isn't much distance between my bedroom-slash-living-room and the kitchen. It's only a few steps to turn on the coffee machine and warm up the computer before running to the bathroom to take care of morning business and splash some cold water on my face.

By the time that's done, I've got a steaming cup of coffee ready and waiting. I sit in front of my laptop in the small dining space that's also my kitchen and pull up my website and social media accounts.

It's the only apartment I could afford on my own, and there are only three rooms, really. The kitchen-slash-dining-room, the bedroom-slash-living-room and a tremendously tiny bathroom. There's also a closet that's about the same size as the bathroom, but at least they're actual separate rooms.

I'm scanning around, still half awake, when I notice my Twitter followers have increased.

I turn my head just in time to spit my coffee all over the kitchen floor.

"Ten thousand?" I yell into the empty apartment. "Ten *thousand*?"

What happened? I click around and find a tweet of an article with my name in it.

It's been shared almost twenty thousand times.

"Holy shit."

A few more clicks and I find a *Buzzed* article written by Liz Masterson.

Liz was doing the reality show piece; why would she write anything about me?

There's a picture, an old one from a shoot when I was still modeling. Next to it is one of Scarlett at

Miguel's. The headline reads "Former Model Stops a Rape."

I scan through it. Liz wrote a piece about what happened last night. She calls me the Wonder Woman of Broad Street. Snorting a laugh, I click to my blog. Thousands more followers there, too.

What the fuck?

My email box has exploded with job offers. Most of them are still of the celeb "please shoot my wedding/child/family photos" variety, but they're jobs. More than I could ever accept and enough to cover my rent for a while for sure.

Maybe this month I'll spring for the fancy ramen noodles in the big pack.

I power on my phone, and there are a ton of missed calls and messages there, too. I groan. I need an assistant. Half those calls are probably media outlets that I do not want to call back.

Been there, done that.

In between all the job offers is another rejection from a high-profile political rag, which puts a damper on my excitement. I've been pitching my idea for a year now and can't even get a bite.

There's a light tap at my door and I get up and open it without looking through the peephole.

"Hey, Martha." I dash back to my computer, absorbed by the magic happening on my laptop.

"Good morning, dearie." Martha steps into my kitchen, shutting the door behind her and heading straight for my coffee pot.

Martha is my neighbor. She's about ninety years old and comes over every morning to drink my coffee. She also steals weird things like Q-tips, garbage bags, and tampons. Even though I'm pretty sure she hasn't PMS'd in at least forty years. I'm not sure why she takes my things, but I just let her. She bakes me cookies sometimes, so it's a fair trade.

"Are you busy today?"

I glance over at the question. She's wearing her trademark pink floral nightgown and her hair is in curlers. It's always in curlers. "Um, sort of. I have a bunch of new followers on social media."

She blinks. "Oh. Can I use your bathroom?"

"Sure, Martha."

She disappears into my bathroom for so long I nearly forget she's there. Then she's out the door without so much as a goodbye, the pockets of her gown bulging.

I laugh. No matter how "famous" I might be, some things will never change.

An hour later I'm still clicking around online, amazed at all the sudden publicity, when my phone rings, and this time I recognize the number.

"Victoria?" I answer. I haven't talked to her since the Times Square photo. She's the reason I got the job in the first place, but after everything that happened since. . .

"Are you free today? We have a shoot in Harlem. 'New York's Sexiest.' It's for *Stylz*."

In true Victoria fashion, she acts as if nothing's happened and it was only yesterday she was talking me up and promising me the world.

I don't really want to do it. *Stylz* magazine is the same magazine that printed the article describing my shame to the world. But I'm over it. I'm not letting my past drag me down. Again. Even though it's more celebrity nonsense, I would be a fool to say no.

Everyone knows Victoria. Turning her down now would be professional suicide.

"What time?"

Chapter Two

Life, for people, begins to crumble on the edges;
they don't realize it.
                    –Dorothea Lange

Marc

My father has the uncanny ability to take a decent day and turn it into a shit sandwich.

"Do you have those TPS reports?"

"Hello, Dad. Good morning to you, too."

It's almost afternoon. I left work last night at eleven, and I was back in the door seven hours later. He probably wandered in a few minutes ago and expects the world to fall at his feet.

Story of my life.

I'm too exhausted to deal with him.

I can't see my father through the phone, but I can picture him at his desk. I'm sure he's dressed in an Armani suit that costs more than the GDP of a small country, and he likely still reeks of booze from the night before. While I was here, working late into the evening, he was out schmoozing some clients that flew in from China. I'd bet my left foot he hasn't even looked at his desk yet to see if I gave him his damn reports.

"What?" he barks in response to my greeting.

"I put them on your desk before I left last night."

Muttered curses fill my ear and the shuffle of paper crinkles in the background. His desk is always a hurricane of reports and paperwork that he can barely read anymore, let alone keep track of.

I don't know why he bothers coming in at all. He doesn't do anything but bluster and curse and freak out the administrative staff. He's never been good at anything that doesn't require charming people out of their money with fancy dinners and pretty women.

I wait, tense and still, wondering what he'll want next.

There's a click when he hangs up on me without another word, and I release a sigh into the silence. I put the phone back on its base and look out the bank of windows into the city.

I'm on the top floor of one of the biggest corporations in New York City. It's a dream job, really. For anyone else. My grandfather was an immigrant from Scotland and he started the company all by himself when he was in his early twenties. It was a simple enough idea, a one-stop shop for all of the restaurants in the city to purchase kitchen supplies. Now we supply products for thousands of eating establishments across the country, including home stores and giant superstore chains. The company is worth millions.

It was a forgone conclusion that I would work here and eventually take over, especially when my brother Brent began excelling in sports and I had my little accident.

But the truth is, I kind of hate it.

The phone rings. It's not Dad this time but his assistant.

"Marc here."

"Marc, it's Alex."

Poor, poor Alex. My dad sucks, but I'm his child and although technically I'm just an employee with no ownership interest in the company, he wouldn't get rid of me or do anything to hurt me, really. Nothing more than he already does. Alex is the fifth assistant he's had in the last six months. "What's going on?"

"Well, it's about Mr. Crawford."

"It usually is. What is he doing now?"

"He told me only to interrupt him if Dane Jones calls, and well, Dane Jones is on the phone for him."

"Okaaay."

Alex sighs. "Then he shut his door and put his phone on busy. I can hear the music."

Typical Dad behavior. If Alex interrupts him when his music is on, he'll be fired. But if Dad finds out Dane Jones called and Alex didn't interrupt him after he explicitly told him to, he'll be fired.

Dad's a seventy-year-old toddler.

"Ah. I gotcha. Be right there."

We hang up and I take a few deep breaths to prepare myself before I leave the relative safety of my office.

The same thing happens every time I move anywhere inside the building.

"Marc, will you sign this?" Grace stops me, an accountant who's been with the company since I was a child and does the work of ten people while managing to be the office grandmother.

"Can I get you to look at these numbers?" Eric from marketing is next. He's going through a divorce and has been obviously stressed lately. I tell him to leave the reports on my desk.

"Do you think Trina in marketing would go on a date with me?" This from an IT woman I hired last year. Charlie. She hands me a coffee and walks with me.

"Asking out coworkers is a bad idea. And I think she's straight." I take a sip and then frown. Way too much sugar.

She groans. "Why are all the good women taken?"

"When you find out, let me know." I lift the coffee cup in her direction. "Next time, just make it black."

"But you need something sweet in your life." She pats me on the shoulder before disappearing down a hallway.

By the time I make it to Dad's office, Alex is doing a nervous dance outside the door.

I drop my coffee in his trash. "Don't worry, I've got it." I walk past him and open the door without knocking. "Dad, Dane Jones is on the phone." I have to nearly yell the words over the music blaring in the background. Frank Sinatra. He listens to it every time he starts dating someone new. So every other week.

He motions for me to shut off his music and I click the button, thrusting his office into silence.

"Dane Jones is on the phone," I repeat.

With a quick, frustrated breath, he picks up his phone and pushes some buttons. "This thing doesn't work," he grumbles. "Where is that damn secretary of mine? Andrew!"

"His name is Alex."

He points the phone in my direction. "Never heard of a man being a secretary. It's not natural. I don't know why you won't let me pick my own staff."

Because the last two people he hired were blonde and buxom. And while I'm sure they were excellent at their jobs, he immediately started dropping things to make them bend over, kept asking one of them if there was a mirror in her pocket, and gave the other one a dress code with nothing on it. It was literally a list that said *wear nothing*. I don't have time to deal with sexual harassment lawsuits on top of everything else.

But I've learned the best answer to Dad's questions is silence or a subject change.

I walk to his desk and push the button next to the call Alex put on hold. "There."

"Dane," Dad barks into the phone. "Let me call you right back." Then he hangs up on him.

I take a deep breath and count to ten. *I will not kill my father today, I will not kill my father today.*

"Did you finish that paperwork I asked for yesterday?"

The same paperwork you asked me about ten minutes ago? I pick up the bound papers off the corner of his desk and hand it to him. "Yes. It's right here."

He flips through the pages, squinting at the words.

He needs to put on his glasses. He has them, he just refuses to wear them. He avoids anything that would make him look less than a "real man," even when he's only in the company of his son.

Narcissism, thy name is Father.

He finally puts the papers down on his desk. "Why were you here late working? You're young. You should be out partying with your brother. If anyone can pull in the tail, it's him. He could help you out, even with that ugly mug of yours." He laughs at his own joke.

Like I don't realize how I look. After the accident, he pestered me for months about getting plastic surgery for that "horrible disfigurement."

It's just some scars.

I've told him I have a girlfriend about six times. Not that he remembers. I've made a deal with myself that I won't tell him the same thing more than ten times because I'm pretty sure the eleventh time, an angel somewhere gets his wings ripped off.

"Brent's not going out these days. The season started three months ago." Besides that, ever since Bella broke up with Brent, he hasn't had much interest in partying. Not that Dad would know that. Brent and I don't share personal stuff with him. We know better.

"You're right." A sentence that would be surprising if he stopped there. "Brent is getting it done every time he has an away game, I'm sure. He's probably banged a chick in every state. You should learn from your brother." There's more chortling and nudging.

If I had been out partying, I wouldn't have gotten the work done that he wanted and he would have faulted me for that. There's no winning here, only pacifying the beast as best I can.

This place would fall down without me.

Pressure builds behind my eyes. I can't take this much longer. Can a thirty-year-old have a stroke? I take a deep breath and picture myself somewhere else. On a tropical beach. Touring an ancient castle in Europe. Exploring the Great Wall of China.

Anywhere but here.

"Will Brent have time to do those commercials we talked about?" Dad asks.

Brent has become the official spokesperson for the company. Dad's been wanting to open a home and kitchen chain store, starting upstate and eventually branching to the rest of the country. He's been using Brent's star power to get the funding to make it happen.

"He's already done a couple of the ads. We won't need him again until the season is over."

"We really need to get a jump on this if the expansion is going to work."

Which is why I was here until late last night, working out the logistics for exclusivity deals with a few key distributors. Which is what the paperwork I *just* handed him covers. "I'm on it, Dad. I'll let you call Dane back."

I use the excuse to leave his office. A few seconds after I shut his door, the music comes back on.

He'll forget to return Dane's call, and no doubt it will somehow be my fault.

I make it back to my office with only a few interruptions but as soon as I shut the door, my cell rings.

It's Brent.

"Hey," I answer the phone.

"Hey, best brother in the world."

"I'm your only brother in this world."

"Semantics."

"What do you want?"

"What makes you think I want something? Can't I just call my big brother to tell him how awesome he is?" There's soft, measured tapping in the background and I can picture him pacing the living room and tossing his football up and down. It's what he always does. The ball is the same one he got for Christmas when he was ten. He plays with it when he's on the phone or thinking or doing pretty much anything where his hands are free.

"Is that it?" I glance at my watch. "Because I've got to go. Dad's going to be calling me about something ridiculous within the next sixty seconds and while I love hearing about how awesome I am, I'm not sure I have time right now."

"You sound stressed. You need a break and I have just the thing."

"Aha, the truth comes out. What do you want? And why can't we ever start with this?" There's a new stack of paperwork on my desk that wasn't there ten minutes ago. I pick up the top sheet and frown at it. What now?

"I don't want anything from you. I want to help you."

Can he help me with this marketing report that magically appeared out of nowhere? Probably not. "Help me how?"

"Well, you see I have this photo shoot—"

"Okay, let me stop you there with a hard pass. Anything that starts with photo and ends with shoot does not sound like something I am into."

"Hear me out. It's for the sexiest people in New York. There will be a ton of hot babes."

"I don't need babes, I have Marissa." We haven't been dating long, a couple of months, but she's the first girl I've met that doesn't give me a hard time for having to work every day and also hasn't made a pass at my brother.

He's quiet for a few seconds. "Right, well she might be there, too. I think *Stylz* is doing an article about someone."

He's been acting off every time I bring up Marissa. "Do you not like—"

The office phone rings, cutting me off. I glance over at the name on the screen. Albert Crawford. And there's the call from Dad I knew was coming. The headache behind my eyes makes a comeback, flickering to life like a big-screen villain who just won't die.

"What time is this shoot?"

Chapter Three

I was invited to photograph Hollywood. They asked me what I would like to photograph. I said, Ugly men.

–Imogen Cunningham

Gwen

Victoria's photo shoot is on 123rd in East Harlem at some repurposed warehouse rented out for these kinds of things. There are multiple rooms and lots of space, so they lease it out to a variety of 'zines and papers. I have to take a cab with all my equipment and it takes thirty minutes due to the traffic on Martin Luther King Blvd and even though I tell the driver to take 128th, he doesn't listen.

He drops me at the door and it takes me a couple minutes to pull out my heavy case, during which time I get honked at twice and flipped off three times.

Gotta love big-city living.

The space is on the seventh floor, and of course the elevator is broken.

"Why did I wear heels today?" I ask the faded pink walls after I've trudged up the first three flights. The walls don't respond to my bitchy tone. I clutch my camera closer and keep hiking, tempted to pull the heels off, but when I pass a dead rat on one of the steps, that idea is quashed.

When I finally reach the floor in question, my feet are sobbing in pain and my bag is digging into my shoulder like I'm carrying the sun instead of my tripod, battery packs, and lenses. I stop at the door, leaning down a little to catch my breath before I enter the shooting area, which I know will be a chaotic mess of makeup artists, reporters, assistants, PR people, models, and celebrities.

I'm about to stand up when the door swings open, knocking into my arm and sending my camera flying.

"No!" I lunge after the camera—basically my entire world—and everything goes into slow motion. I'm not going to catch it in time, but then an arm reaches out of nowhere and grabs it before it can shatter all over the ground.

"I'm so sorry," a masculine voice says.

"Oh!" My gaze is completely focused on my camera, still intact, in the stranger's hand. My mind is still flashing images of exploding camera parts as it hits the ground. I can't believe it's okay.

I reach for it. He hands it over. It isn't until the device is safely in my grasp that I look up and meet his eyes.

Then everything stops.

It isn't like the movies. Not really. There's no music or choir of singing angels. But something happens in that moment.

He's *interesting*.

The first thing I notice are the scars. There's a deep gash that starts above his right eye and follows the curve of his eyebrow down, making a sharp turn toward his cheek. There are more lines, smaller marks that shoot down his right cheek. His hair is dark and trimmed, and his face is clean-shaven. His blue eyes are offset by dark eyebrows—one of which is creased by the scar—and there's a slight divot between his eyes as he watches me. His lips are on the thin side and slightly crooked, his nose is overlarge, and as a complete package he's entirely average, but there's a depth in his eyes. And kindness. It's a compelling mixture that's completely—holy crap, do I need to get laid?

But no, it's not like that. It's not that I'm attracted to him per se. And yet . . .

"Can I photograph you?" The words blurt out of my mouth like a gush of water from a fire hydrant in July, entirely out of my control.

He blinks and steps back, the crease between his brow deepening as he regards me in surprise. "I'm not a model."

"Oh, I know that," I say and then immediately regret the words and what they imply. "I mean, not that I don't think you're," one hand flails in his direction. "I just mean you look . . ."

I'm killing this conversation slowly.

Heat creeps up my neck as I flounder for words.

He laughs, the sound awkward and full of self-deprecatory amusement. "I hold no false illusions about my appearance."

My mouth opens again, likely to say something even worse, but thankfully he rescues me with a wave of his hand.

"Don't worry, no offense taken. I'm here giving moral support to my brother, Brent Crawford."

I nod in recognition. Brent Crawford. Newest rookie for the New York Sharks, second-round draft pick, and widely regarded as the newest Johnny Football this season. They've been calling him Superman. Also a young, attractive bachelor that's been making every female in a two-hundred-mile radius lose their minds and toss their panties in his general direction while screaming and fainting as if they're auditioning for an on-Broadway performance of *Hard Day's Night*.

"I'm Gwen McDougall." I hold out my non-camera-holding hand and he shakes it.

"Marc Crawford. Here, let me help you with your bag." He easily pulls the heavy equipment bag off my shoulder.

"Thank you," I say, surprised at the chivalry. He hasn't even glanced down at my tits once. This has got to be some kind of record.

In contrast, while he's adjusting my bag on his own shoulder, I shamelessly check him out more. The irony that *I'm* objectifying *him* is not lost on me.

It's not in a sexual way. It's art.

Or so I tell myself.

He's wearing a suit, but he looks good under the professional cut of his jacket and button-up shirt. Not as fit as his footballer brother, but not bad. He's shorter, too. We're about the same height and I'm wearing two-inch heels, which puts him at about five foot ten.

"You don't look like your brother."

"That's the understatement of the year." A bit of red is creeping up his neck and there's a mirroring heat in my own face.

Why can't I talk to this guy without insulting him? "I didn't mean it like that," I try to explain. "I was serious about wanting to take your picture."

He watches my face, scanning my eyes while his own are full of bafflement. "Why? Because of this?" He points a finger to the scarred side of his face.

My eyes track over where he's pointing and I shrug. "Chicks dig scars."

He barks out a laugh and opens the door from the stairwell. "I can't say I've ever had anyone use that phrase in reference to me." We walk down the hall toward the sound of bustling people. "I don't have an interesting face."

There's something in his voice that stops me. It's like when an abused child puts themselves down because it's what they've always heard, but they're really dying for approval.

I put a hand on his arm. "But you really do. Your face might not be the societal ideal for beauty, but you have obvious character that most people lack. Especially beautiful people."

He glances down at my hand and then back up at my face, already shaking his head, confusion flickering in his eyes. He opens his mouth to speak.

The door behind us slams open against the wall, making us both turn at the sound. "There you are! Did you know the elevator was broken? What is wrong with people that they can't get their buildings fixed?"

The screechy voice is familiar. I grip my camera tighter, as if it could protect me. Marissa Reeves, reporter for the gossip rag *Stylz*. I could never prove it but I'm nearly certain that she was the one behind the article they ran about me a year ago.

She's a psycho hose beast.

She walks right up, pushing herself between us and knocking my hand off his arm—I didn't even realize it was still there—and then she kisses my new friend on his perfectly imperfect mouth.

~*~

25

I don't meet Brent Crawford until nearly two hours later. I love photography, but most of this celeb racket is for the birds. And not pretty birds like peacocks, but dumpster birds who screech and claw and offer no real benefit to the planet.

"I can't work under these conditions," complains an A-list star, one who stars in a ton of action movies and does his own stunts and by all reports is "a great guy." The problem? We don't have the brand of water he prefers.

I glance around for Victoria. There's been too much activity, trying to get all the shots done in one day. They have the space divvied up into ministudios with various backdrops and fill lights. I only saw Victoria once right after I arrived. She had time to air kiss me on both cheeks and point me in the direction of one of the setups and I haven't seen her since.

It's nice that she trusts me, I guess, but the truth is we have similar if unorthodox shooting methods. We want to get a person's true character instead of the one they wish to present to the world. Which is why, while my celebrity is bitching and distracted, I catch some shots of his true colors. Not sure if the magazine will run the shot of his snarling mouth and cold eyes, but I know Victoria will appreciate it. I have a theory that she gets so many great shoots because of the amount of blackmail material she has.

The celeb's handlers manage to calm him down, and I get a few more decent shots that he won't sue me over. Hopefully.

I thought I would get away from this drama when I left modeling, but apparently not.

Two hours later, and we're nearly finished. Brent is the last shoot of the day, and I brace myself for some possible meltdown behavior.

A majority of the people have left, so the melee has died down a bit. All that's left are a few straggling reporters, a makeup artist, and a stylist who stays on hand in case of emergency.

Brent introduces himself and shakes my hand much like his brother did, which makes me hopeful. Most of these people didn't even bother. I have him sit on the bench in the middle of the set. He's surrounded by stark-white material and I adjust the lights as I walk around him, looking at him from different angles.

I really can't see much of Marc in his features. Brent is taller and wider. His jaw has a harsher angle and his nose is straight and fits his face perfectly. They do have the same dark hair and blue eyes, but while Marc has the world in his eyes, Brent's are somehow lighter. Less serious.

He's wearing a long-sleeved dark grey sweater that fits his form and shows off his physique. The contrast between the dark clothing and white background should make some good shots if I can play up a bit of shadow in the background to emphasize his features. But there's a rigidity to his shoulders and jaw that becomes apparent as I play with the lighting. He's not comfortable in front of the camera, although he puts up a good front.

"I met your brother," I tell Brent as I'm adjusting a tripod. *And completely offended him, numerous times in quick succession, like my mouth is an automatic weapon full of insults.*

"Oh yeah? He's the best. He's still around here somewhere, I think, with his girlfriend."

Something twinges in my chest at the words and I inwardly shake myself.

Why should I care if he's dating a psycho beyotch? I just met him. I don't even know him, even though I obviously stuck my foot in my mouth and was completely rude to him. Maybe the awkwardness is because I have a care for another human in general. I wouldn't wish Marissa Reeves on my worst enemy.

"Is Marc your only brother or do you have other siblings?" Asking personal, if somewhat inane questions is a trick I use to get people to relax. Everyone loves talking about themselves. And if I can get them talking and comfortable, I can get a sense of who they really are instead of the façade they present to the world.

"Just me and Marc," he says. "What about you?"

I stop adjusting the light lamp in front of me and find him watching me. He's actually interested in my response.

Not interested like *that*, and even if he were, I don't date pretty boys or celebrities. Not anymore. But he's looking at me like he actually cares about my answer. Which isn't normal in this business.

"I have two sisters."

"Are they older or younger?" he asks before I can ask him another question to keep him talking.

"They're both older. I'm the baby." I move back behind the camera on the tripod aimed in his direction.

"So we have that in common." The flash of his teeth is dazzling.

I press the shutter a few times and then straighten. "Everyone knows the youngest in the family is always the best one. The first kids are just experiments until they get it right."

That makes him laugh and I snap a few more shots. "Did you want me to pose or look a certain way or something?"

"No. I know that's typical, but candid shots always turn out much better. Relax. Sit however you're most comfortable. We can talk about whatever you want and this'll all be over in a minute."

After a few more shots, it's clear Brent is too wound up to lie around, so I have him stand and move as he pleases for a bit, snapping shots at different angles while we chat.

"How long have you been a photographer?" he asks.

"Not long, a few years."

"Weren't you a model, before?"

"Yeah."

"I think I saw you somewhere." His eyes widen. "No, wait, it was recently. Aren't you the Wonder Woman of Broad Street?"

I laugh and tinker with my camera to hide the heat filling my face. "Hardly. It's not anything special."

"I don't know about that. The article I read was pretty rad."

"Well, you know how those click-bait stories are."

"Oh believe me, I understand unwanted attention." He grimaces and rubs the back of his head and I click the shutter.

"I bet. Aren't you Superman?"

He laughs. "Maybe we should start the Justice League."

"Only if I get to be the Flash," a voice calls out from the other side of the room. Marc walks over to the camera and stops a few feet away, crossing his arms over his chest.

"You are way too slow to be the Flash," Brent teases.

"I am not slow."

"You are."

"I'm methodical. There's a difference."

"Don't listen to him, Gwen. When we were kids, on our birthdays every year, our mom would give us a set amount of money to spend at any store we wanted. I would blow through my hundred-dollar allowance in five minutes. This guy," he jerks a thumb in Marc's direction, "would take hours figuring out what he wanted and calculating the costs and comparing one toy with another."

"There's nothing wrong with making sure you know what you want."

"There's nothing right with it either."

They both laugh and I smile because the cadence is almost exactly the same. Brent's shoulders aren't as rigid as they were before. I snap a few pictures while they laugh together.

We chat and I continue taking pictures. Brent asks about the rest of the shots and how they went. I tell them stories of some diva meltdowns—without names, although I'm sure they can figure it out—and then the conversation turns into a reflection on the strangeness of our semicelebrity lives.

"It's like people who are in the thick of it start to have a distorted view of reality. You know what I mean?" I ask.

I've never really been able to form this into words. My family would never get it. They live normal lives with normal jobs, without the worry of being a public specter or fodder for the masses.

"And then there's the worry about falling from grace," Brent says.

"Yeah, I've been there," I admit with a small laugh.

"It's like living in a fantasy land where you can't distinguish between what's fake and what's real."

"Or who's fake and who's real."

We meet eyes and share a moment of commiseration. I never thought that today I would find someone who understands what things are really like. Everyone else is stuck in the fantasy.

"I feel so bad for you beautiful people," Marc says drily. "It must be hard having more stalkers than Katy Perry has Twitter followers."

"Stalkers?" I raise a brow. "I don't have any stalkers. That I know of."

"Brent has a bunch. One sends him these creepy serial-killer letters. They even use this ancient-looking vellum and fancy ink. We had to send it to the cops to have them analyze it. They said it takes a significant amount of time to write up even one. He's gotten like fifty."

"That is pretty creepy."

"Oh it gets worse," Marc says. "They even sent him pictures of dead chickens."

I laugh. "Dead chickens? Why?"

"Who knows?" Brent says. "Someone with a mental illness, more than likely. You know how it is. Sometimes people think they know you but they really only know what they read and see on TV. They create a whole version of reality in their heads."

"Kind of like some of the celebrities we know," I say.

"Two sides of the same coin," Brent agrees.

A door slams nearby and a voice screeches out over the open space. "Brent, you look so great!"

Marissa is back. Why is she always slamming things? Probably for attention. I bet she's a scream-sneezer.

She walks over to Marc and links her arm through his, murmuring something in his ear that makes him smile.

They talk for a minute, their heads huddled together and I can't make out the words, just the low sound of voices.

I focus on Brent inside the viewfinder. He's frowning and watching his brother.

I wonder why.

The shrieky pitch of Marissa's voice knifes into my ears again. "I have to go, but I'll see you Friday night for dinner?"

Marc nods and she kisses him on the cheek, leaving behind a streak of red.

"Bye, Brent!" she calls as she's leaving, completely ignoring me. Not that I care. I'm used to it.

And from the likes of her, I'm grateful for it.

Chapter Four

*I suffered evils, but without allowing them to
rob me of the freedom to expand.*
        –Gordon Parks

Marc

"I'm sorry but I'm going to be late for dinner. We'll have to cancel our reservations." It's seven thirty on Friday night. I should have been out of here by five, but I've spent the last two hours fixing a report Dad completely screwed up. "I have at least another hour here. But you don't have to wait for me. We can go out tomorrow."

"I haven't seen you since the shoot on Monday," Marissa says, her voice pouty. "I can wait at your apartment. Maybe that will entice you to hurry. Brent can let me in, right?"

I hesitate. Is her tone calculating, or am I just tired? "Yes, Brent's there."

"Great. I'll head over there in a little while. Let me know when you're on your way and I can order takeout or something. My treat."

"That sounds great." I relax.

We hang up and I frown at my computer. Time to get to work.

But I can't focus, thinking about Marissa. Brent's been acting weird about her lately. Well, not exactly weird, just silent. And I know Brent well enough to know something is up, but I'm not sure what. If it was something serious, surely he would have said something.

And now she will be there waiting for me. With him.

I'm paranoid. But I have reason to be. She wouldn't be the first woman I dated who was more interested in my brother than me.

But Marissa is different. She never asks me questions about Brent. She hardly even mentions him.

Except for the other night. After the photo shoot in Harlem, she called to ask if everything was okay with Brent and the photographer. Apparently there was some scandal with Gwen over a year ago, and Marissa was worried about Brent getting involved.

When I asked Brent about Gwen, he said nothing had happened. They hadn't even exchanged numbers. Then he asked why I wanted to know, and if I had heard anything about her, and was she single. It's the most interest I've seen him show in a girl since Bella broke up with him. But odds are we'll never see her again.

The thought makes me frown. Her face was sincere when she asked to take my picture, even though every other word out of her mouth was a direct hit.

I chuckle, remembering the look on her face when she said she knew I wasn't a model. So full of chagrin and embarrassment. An oddly sweet mixture.

While no one should be shocked that I'm not a model, it's equally unshocking that Gwen is a former model. She has the trademarks of someone who stepped off the runway, all long and lean—except not quite as waifish—with perfectly sculpted features.

When I asked Marissa why Gwen was bad news, she only said Gwen was flighty and naïve and Brent was better off without her. But Gwen didn't come off that way, not in the few minutes we spent chatting.

Marissa's warning piqued my interest enough that I took the time to google Gwen McDougall. A bunch of old articles came up in the search feed. She was the hot new thing for a fashion line one year, and in the next she had moved behind the camera and one of her shots was front and center in Times Square. Then a few months after that, an article in *Stylz*, Marissa's magazine, stated that Gwen had had some kind of meltdown and couldn't handle the pressures of her new job. Sources close to her had said she was unreliable, perhaps faking her success—no information about how she pulled that off exactly, which made me think it was bunk. Though, her boyfriend and best friend were quoted saying that she'd cracked and gone off the deep end.

I can't quite fit the allegations in the article with the woman I met. Then again, this article is over a year old. People change. Besides, everyone is entitled to a little meltdown every now and then. I don't know why this one thing makes Marissa so concerned about Gwen and Brent but . . . whatever.

I shrug the thoughts off and focus. I have to get this work done so I can get out of here.

Over two hours later, I'm done fixing the report numbers and charts and everything else. Dad really needs to retire, but as long as he's having fun partying, I don't think he'll ever give it up. Which means I'll be spending the next however many years trailing behind him with a virtual DustBuster, cleaning up his mess.

Anxious to be home, knowing Marissa is waiting, I call down to the lobby for a company car.

I wave to the security guards as I jog past them to the elevators.

I'm in such a hurry that I don't realize until I'm halfway down Lexington that I forgot my cell back at the office.

"Dammit." I didn't call Marissa to let her know, but it's too late now.

I nod at the doorman while speed walking to yet another elevator. The ride up is twice as long as normal.

Everything feels off, but I can't pinpoint the reason.

When I get to our floor, instead of rushing into the apartment, I take my time and open the door quietly, stepping inside and shutting it behind me without a sound.

Voices come from the living room.

"Come on Brent, Marc will never know." It's Marissa, speaking with a teasing lilt I haven't heard before.

I freeze in the hallway. I can't see them, but I can hear Brent's response.

"Marissa. Stop. Marc is my brother. Besides, I've told you before. I'm not interested."

Before?

And immediately after that thought, *Again?*

I should have seen it coming. Maybe a part of me did see it coming, hence the creeping in the entryway like a stalker.

The problem is that I always want to believe that this time . . . this time, a girl will want me for me and not my attractive and athletic brother.

When will I learn?

I shake my head and take a deep breath to thaw out my frozen limbs.

"Hey, guys." I stop in the doorway from the entry to the living room.

Brent is standing, arms crossed, behind the recliner in the corner. His jaw is tense and his eyes swing toward me, full of apology and something else I can't stand. Pity.

Marissa is on the recliner, facing him, and she's naked. Her head spins around and her mouth gapes opens. I half expect her eyes to pop out of her head and roll away like a cartoon.

"You were supposed to call before you left the office."

I almost laugh. "Well. I'm real sorry about that, Marissa."

I wait to see if she's going to get the irony of my apology, considering she's sitting there naked and propositioning my brother, but the moment doesn't come.

Instead, it's just silence. They're both looking at me and I'm looking around the room. "Where are your clothes?"

"What? That's all you have to say? You don't even care that your brother, that he, that he—"

"That he what? Turned you down?"

She stands and crosses her arms over her chest. It's not a bad chest, I've enjoyed it myself a few times over the last couple of months, but at this point I can barely stand to look at her. Even my inner caveman, who loves looking at boobs, won't take a minute to enjoy the view. My stomach is churning.

"Put your clothes on and leave."

"You can't tell me what to do. No one can," she snaps. But she does move, stomping down the hall in the direction of the bedrooms. She left her clothes in there?

"Marc . . ." says Brent.

"Not now." I take a few steps into the living room and drop into the plush leather sofa, resting my elbows on my knees and my face in my hands.

I want nothing more than to go hide in my room, but I have to wait until Marissa gets dressed and I have no idea which room she left her clothes in, Brent's or mine. And how did she ever think I wouldn't find out? Although, Brent did say he'd told her before. How many times has she thrown herself at him? And why didn't he tell me?

The clomping of her feet heralds her return. Her clothes have been yanked on, topped with a scowl on her face. "You guys suck." She stomps toward the door and I wait to hear the door slam, but instead there's silence for a few long seconds. Brent and I lock gazes, waiting. Then there's a big crash right before the front door opens and then slams shut.

"She broke the Japanese vase," Brent says.

"Yep."

"I need a drink." He disappears into the kitchen and a couple moments later reemerges with two open beers in his hands.

He passes me one and I take a long drink. "I need something stronger."

He moves to the small bar in the corner and opens the scotch, bringing me a small glass before sitting next to me on the plush couch.

Dad's designer furnished the apartment for me. Brent moved in when Bella left and he couldn't stand being alone. It made sense, since we're both rarely here anyway. There are three bedrooms and every amenity you could ever need, including a gym for Brent to work out in the off-season. It's wasteful to have two barely used apartments when we can comfortably live in the same one and still rarely see each other. I'm rethinking that decision, though.

"Why didn't you tell me?"

"I'm sorry, man. I was going to, but the last time she tried something, she was drunk and I thought it didn't mean anything. I shrugged it off and she never mentioned it so I thought she forgot. It was not like this. And after Cynthia . . ." He runs a hand through his hair and grimaces.

He won't say it outright, but the last girlfriend I had was also using me to get to Brent and didn't even bother hiding it after the first couple of dates.

"At least you know now," he says. "Better to find out someone's true colors early on. She's gone for good."

The words are supposed to make me feel better, and in a way, they do. But another part of me is supremely disappointed. Not necessarily that Marissa is gone. We'd only been dating a couple months, and thanks to my work, we barely saw each other as it was.

My heart's not broken because of her.

What hurts more are the self-defeating thoughts. Will I ever find someone who wants me and not him? Will I always be in my brother's shadow? Will I always have to worry that anyone I end up with would rather be with him? I'm not as hot as he is. I know it. I'm not as athletic, famous, or even as wealthy as Brent.

Why would anyone pick me?

~*~

The next morning, I'm in the kitchen making a cup of coffee when Brent appears in the doorway, holding his laptop. "Remember how I said Marissa was gone for good?" He turns it around so I can see the screen. "I lied."

"What is that?" It's some kind of web article. There's a picture of him at the top of the page, but I can't make out the words.

I walk closer and read the words out loud. "Brent Crawford—Superman or super sexual . . . *predator*?" My brows lift and I meet his eyes, taking in his pale face and shocked expression.

"The picture is from that night she was drunk and came on to me."

It's not a clear shot, but from all appearances she's passed out and he's leaning over her.

"Based on the angle, her phone must have been on the table by the couch. She hit on me and then I helped her into an Uber. I had to practically carry her downstairs. That pic must have been taken when I was helping her up." He sighs and shakes his head. "The article says that I came on to her and then blamed her when you walked in on us."

I grab the laptop and put it on the counter so I can skim down the words, my heart pounding with the implications. This could ruin Brent's career. And tank the company. The amount Dad's insisted we sink into this retail rollout is not something I want to contemplate right now, but if I don't, who will? "This is all my fault." Marissa planned these shots, weeks ago. How did I not see what she was really about? How could I miss it?

"It's not your fault she's crazy. You didn't publish these pictures."

"No, but I decided to date her and let her into our lives. I should have seen it sooner. You saw it sooner. Why didn't you say something?"

"I didn't see this. I knew she wasn't the one for you, but I didn't think she would stoop to something so . . .

damaging to our whole family. There's no one to blame here but the real culprit. Marissa."

He's not blaming me, but the words hurt because they're true. "I'll contact the paper."

"It won't matter. Even if they print a retraction, it'll be in fine print on the last page." He winces. "Starlee is going to kill me. Dad is going to kill me. I'm supposed to be the all-American poster boy for the company, not . . ." He runs a frustrated hand through his hair. "Whatever this is."

"I'm surprised Starlee hasn't—"

Brent's phone chirps. He pulls it out of his pocket and looks at the display, lifting his brows.

"—called yet."

As he turns away to answer the call, I turn my focus back on the coffee maker. "Hi, Starlee," he says.

Brent winces and holds the phone away from his ear while Starlee screeches on the other end. I can't quite make out the words, only the volume. The shouting stops suddenly.

"She's coming over," Brent explains. "She said don't talk to anyone."

Within minutes she's at the door, fresh-faced and raring to go.

We're still sitting in the living room in our robes and underwear, silent, too shocked to process anything.

"We need a plan, like now, like five minutes ago, like three days ago." Starlee is five feet two inches of terror packed into a smart black suit. She operates on only two levels of emotion. If she's not at a ten, she's at a twelve. But I guess, being one of only a handful of female sports agents, she doesn't have much of a choice. It's always about proving herself.

"Three of your sponsors are already talking about pulling out and the Sharks issued a statement that they're going to open an internal investigation, which could result in a suspension." She puts her briefcase on the counter and clicks it open. "What did you do to piss off crazy-pants Marissa Reeves?"

"Crazy pants?" Brent asks.

"Yeah." She pulls out her copy of the magazine and flips it open to the article in question. "It's what everyone calls her. She's nuts. Why didn't you tell me you were dating her?"

"I wasn't dating her, Marc was dating her."

"Marc," she barks.

I shrug. "I didn't know she was crazy. I don't put much stock into rumors and hearsay."

"Well. Done but can't be undone. Now we have to fix it. What happened?"

Brent explains the details of our evening and how he thinks she got the photo.

"Okay." She taps a finger against her lips. "I'll issue a statement. We're going to say that you fully support and will cooperate with any investigation the Sharks want to pursue."

"Of course," Brent says.

"I'm also going to mention that Marissa hasn't filed any charges and get some people tweeting about that little nugget to help sway some of the media in your favor." She shakes her head and sighs. "I doubt she'll go there. Knowing Marissa, she doesn't want legal fees, just media attention. And then we need to work on recovering your good boy image. You need a girlfriend quick. A good girlfriend. Someone famous, but not too famous. Hot, but likeable. Someone people like a lot. America's-sweetheart type. You know anyone?"

Brent glances over at me and then back at Starlee and shrugs.

I clear my throat. "I think I might."

Chapter Five

*A thing that you see in my pictures is that I
was not afraid to fall in love with these people.*
    –Annie Leibovitz

Gwen

"Holy crap," I murmur and take a sip of my coffee,
skimming the article about Brent in *Stylz*. "Sexual
predator?"

I only met Brent once, but he was . . . not smarmy. I
can't believe it. The man could get anyone he wants with
his fame and money and good looks alone, plus he's
funny and nice. It's like finding a rainbow-colored
unicorn in the middle of Manhattan.

Not that that means anything. I shouldn't let my
own issues with Marissa affect my thoughts about an
allegation of this nature. Crappy people get assaulted,
too. But I can't help wondering . . .

Is Marissa lying?

Why would she lie?

I grimace at the photos in the article. He's just
standing there. How did she get these shots anyway? It
looks like a camera phone, maybe with some kind of
timer.

There was a B-list actor, a couple years ago, that she
became obsessed with. Lucky told me the story, so I have

to take it with a grain of salt, but apparently she followed the guy one night when he was on a date, all the way back to his apartment and listened to him hooking up with someone else at the door.

She had a weird thing for Lucky, too, which is why I think she printed the article about me. There's no doubt she's got a screw loose.

Did she switch her fixation to Brent? I've never seen her print something like this, though.

I don't have time to think about Marissa very long because my phone and email start going crazier than she is. I've already responded to some of the jobs I can't do—mostly the personal shoots, I need more professional jobs to bulk up my portfolio—and I schedule out the stuff I want to work on for the next two weeks.

Things are finally taking off and I have my own little fifteen minutes of fame to thank.

Except . . . I got yet another rejection. I've been trying to get someone to listen to my idea for a photo essay and I keep getting doors shut in my face.

It's bad enough that editors take one look at me and assume I'm a ditzy blonde; toting around nothing more than celebrity shots and models in my portfolio is like having herpes. I guess I should be grateful they even took the time to respond with their rejection.

I've been pitching the idea of an inside look into endangered cultures around the world. I want to start with the Kalash, an indigenous people who've managed to retain and practice their unique religion, customs, and traditions despite being nestled in the middle of predominantly Muslim Pakistan. There are only three thousand Kalash left. And that's just a jumping-off point. There are so many cultures around the world that are rapidly disappearing under an onslaught of technological advancement and encroaching settlements. Someone has to capture them while we still can. And I want that someone to be me.

I was hoping since the Wonder Woman article went viral that I would have a better chance for an interview at least.

No matter, there are other magazines and I'm going to apply to all of them. Someone will listen, eventually.

In the afternoon I'm running from one job to another when I get yet another call.

"Gwen McDougall," I answer.

"Gwen, this is Starlee Miller. We've met before, at a charity event a couple years ago."

I mentally rack my brain. Starlee Miller. Petite, dark hair, her husband works for *News Weekly*, a popular political rag. I only remember her because of her spouse, actually. His best friend is Warren Bateman, a Pulitzer Prize–winning photographer.

"Right. The Children's Hospital gala."

"Yes." She sounds surprised that I remember her. "I was wondering if we could meet sometime today. I have an offer for you that I need to talk to you about in person."

I have to admit, I'm curious. And even though she's only indirectly associated with someone I greatly admire and would love to meet, in this industry, it isn't only about talent. It's about who you know, regardless of what people like to say in interviews and print. If I could get someone to put in a good word, maybe I'd have a chance.

"I'm heading to a shoot this afternoon, but I can meet you after. Say six?"

"Great. McClaren's on Fifty-Fifth, you know it?"

"I do." An Irish pub with your typical bar fare, but nice ambience.

We agree to meet and then hang up.

I don't have much time to ponder the conversation or what Starlee Miller might want from me because my afternoon is filled with shoots for an article in *Page Seven* and a few personal photography sessions I scheduled prior to the viral article.

I race home to drop off everything but my camera and case and then I take a cab to McClaren's, arriving just in time.

McClaren's is located in a narrow brick building in Hell's Kitchen. Three floors are peppered with deep red booths, lots of wood paneling, and a shiny brown wood bar on each floor. It's one of those places where businessmen meet after hours to talk shop, loosen their ties, and call the pretty waitresses "sweetheart." When I give the hostess my name, she takes me up the staircase in the back to the second floor, where it's less crowded.

Starlee is already waiting for me at a small booth near the back. She looks like I remember, a small woman in her mid-forties with dark hair and an expensive, but simple suit.

She stands and shakes my hand. "It's nice to see you again."

"You, too."

As soon as I sit across from her, the waitress appears as if she'd been waiting for me to arrive.

We order drinks and then Starlee immediately gets down to business. "I understand you recently met one of my clients, Brent Crawford."

It doesn't take much for me to put the pieces together. "Is this about the story in *Stylz* that hit this morning?"

She nods. "It is."

I lean back in the booth and consider her. If she's going to be blunt, I might as well be, too. "What do you want from me?"

"I know you've been bit in the ass by Marissa before. You've done a great job digging yourself back out, and with the recent bit of notoriety you've gotten, anything that happened over a year ago is forgotten."

"Nothing like that ever completely dies."

She waves a hand. "Everyone knows you were the victim in that situation, despite Marissa's efforts. The only reason she still has her job is because she can sell stories, real or imagined. You are perfect for what Brent needs."

"And what does Brent need?"

"A girlfriend."

I consider her words. It makes sense. Marissa is accusing him of being a predator, I took down a predator. Nothing would hit back at her false accusations faster than Brent dating me.

And it would burst Marissa's bubble, which is a bonus.

But . . .

"Listen, Starlee. I know Marissa and how she is. But I've only met Brent once. And while Marissa isn't my favorite person, that doesn't mean she's lying. I can't even entertain doing something like this without being one hundred percent convinced that he's innocent."

The waitress comes back with our beers and Starlee doesn't respond to my comment until she's dropped off the drinks and walked back out of earshot. "What I'm about to tell you remains completely off the record."

"Okay."

She takes a long drink of her beer and puts her cup down carefully before meeting my eyes. "Brent is impotent."

Shock slaps me back in my seat. "Um, how do you . . ."

"There are medical records. I've already had a signed affidavit drawn up, which I will send to you with an NDA if you agree to help him out. Brent signed a medical release as well, so you can call his doctor and confirm. You won't have full access to his medical, just enough to convince you he's not lying."

I stare at her for a minute. I don't know what to say. "Just because he can't ... you know, doesn't mean he didn't assault Marissa."

She pulls the magazine from the briefcase on the seat next to her, already opened to Marissa's article, and puts it on the table in front of me. A sentence has been highlighted that says Brent took every opportunity to show Marissa his erect penis and told her he would "bone her all night long."

Pretty obviously a lie if what Starlee is saying is true, which apparently it is if she's offering up medical evidence to support it.

"Why doesn't Brent tell the truth, to the media? If he has medical records to prove it?"

Her head is shaking before I even finish the sentence. "No one knows about Brent's condition except me and his doctors. And now you. I was out of the loop myself until this morning. Marc doesn't even know." She shakes her head and releases a heavy sigh. "The only reason Brent told me was because he wanted you to be assured."

Huh.

"I tried to get him to go public with the medical but he won't tell me everything that's going on. Only that he's having this ... side effect. I don't think he fully understands the ramifications of an allegation like this so early in his career. It's a financial disaster. Who knows how long his career will last? A physical injury could end it at any time, which means gaining celebrity traction is essential to keep the endorsement money rolling in if and when he has to retire."

I nod in acknowledgement. As his agent, she would be worried about the money because that's where she gets her cut.

But do I really want to do this whole fake relationship thing? Brent's obviously got a lot on his plate, and a shallow, vindictive part of me would love to stick it to Marissa. I know these "arrangements" happen all the time behind the scenes in this bubble of celebrity un-reality, but it feels so . . . underhanded. Besides, putting myself back into the limelight isn't what I want, not this kind of attention. This won't help me with my career.

Starlee watches me carefully while speaking her next words. "You know, I've heard you've been pitching an idea around town about a potential human-interest piece."

"You've done your homework on me."

"It's my job. My friend Warren works at *News Weekly*."

I freeze, my ears perking up at the words. I've been sending requests every other week to different places for the opportunity to present my idea. I've never even gotten as much as a nibble. "What are you offering?"

"I can't guarantee anything with Warren. But I could put in a word for you. I could even hand over your proposal myself. I also have other connections with magazines in this city. I could get you more than one shot at this."

It's not a promise, but it's an opportunity. The opportunity I've been waiting for — to get someone to look past my blonde hair and modeling history and give me a shot at something.

I can't believe I'm even considering this, but how could I not? This is what I've been working for.

And besides that, Marissa sucks. Fuck her for lying about assault just to get some notoriety in a magazine. False allegations like hers undermine the real victims and is one of the reasons people are less likely to report.

I don't know Brent well but I felt a connection with him and his brother the other day. And now I feel almost more connected, knowing his secret, knowing he's been holding this inside for however long and only released the information to gain my trust.

He's not like a majority of the people I've met in the industry.

Then again, can I trust my instincts? I thought the same thing about Lucky and Becca and I got completely fucked over.

"If you would put in a word for me with Warren, I will do something to help Brent. For a short time."

"Thank you." She smiles warmly at me before getting back to business. "I'll send over a contract to sign along with the medical information. Standard nondisclosure with an option to cancel but not for at least three weeks. Marc knows about the fake relationship, but that's it."

I nod like I've done this before but I have no idea. I'll have to read it over carefully once I get it.

We talk about Brent's schedule—the football season has started, so we'll have to work around his away games and it's likely I'll have to make appearances at a home game at the very least. She adds some information about a kids club he and Marc volunteer at.

"Since Brent is on the road a lot over the next few months, only Marc will be there most of the time. Right now he's getting a website done up for them. We can put your name as the photographer for the photos on the site.

It will look good if people start digging, plus it'll strengthen the cause. The charity is a family tradition, so we might as well get some positive exposure for it as a silver lining from all this mess."

"I'm not putting my name on something I haven't done. Send me the details for the kids club and I'll make time this week to stop by and take some pictures."

She tilts her head in acknowledgement. "I think we're going to work together on this just fine, Ms. McDougall. Now. For the first date out in public."

Brent and I will have our first outing tomorrow night. Dinner. A car will pick me and Brent up and take us somewhere there are sure to be a few paparazzi lying in wait.

Throughout the conversation my thoughts drift back to Marc. Everyone is so concerned with the Brent backlash, but what about Marc? He must have had his heart broken, too, a nasty side effect of dealing with Marissa.

Who's rushing to his side while I'm at Brent's?

~*~

Brent lives in Greenwich Village at The Nathaniel, a place so fancy it's got its own human name. It's one of those places with a wall of sparkling windows at the entrance and a rotating door. Inside, the front lobby is sleek, polished, and awash in doormen.

Doormen!

All I have is a homeless guy who passes out in front of my building every night and leaves a trail of urine that stretches to the street.

Apparently, they are expecting me because a doorman directs me to Brent's floor.

I had to dress the part for the date. It's been a while since I got myself all gussied up for cameras. Thankfully, I have some fashionable attire and makeup leftover from my glory days. It's weird, though. Sort of like putting on a mask. And the dress is on the tight side. I've gained a few pounds since I'm not being pressured into starving myself anymore.

I find his apartment—on the top floor, of course—with ease and after a deep breath, I knock three times.

There's shuffling on the other side of the door and then it swings open.

"Hey." It's Marc.

"It's you," I blurt.

He's dressed casually in jeans and a T-shirt. He has slight grey smudges under his eyes, but other than that he's clean-shaven and put together. He doesn't look like I did after my last breakup, like I just crawled out of a garbage can, so there's that.

But I can't help but wonder. Did he lose sleep because of what happened with Marissa?

I don't generally hate people, but that chick needs to be taken down. Or put in a facility for the mentally deranged and totally bitchy.

He smiles when he sees me, the expression reaching his eyes. "It is me."

I glance at the number on the door again, then back into the cavernous space. The entryway is about half the size of my entire apartment. "Is this not Brent's apartment? I could swear Starlee said 1010."

"Oh." Something flickers behind his eyes, darkening them before he holds the door open wider and steps back to let me in. "Yeah. Brent's here. He's getting ready. He —"

"Is she here?" Brent steps out from the hallway into the entry, wearing only slacks, no shirt, exposing his broadly muscled chest and arms. "Hey."

"Hi." I keep my eyes on his face. Brent is extremely well built, no doubt due to hours and hours of training. It doesn't faze me as much as it probably should, since I spent a few years around half-naked models, posing with them, dating them . . . although they tended to be leaner.

More like Marc.

I glance behind me as Marc shuts the door, wondering what Marc might be hiding under his shirt.

"Thank you for doing this." Brent's voice startles me. He's moved closer, right in front of me. "I know it's . . . unconventional. And you don't even know me."

"I know. But I do know Marissa. She's burned me before. I wish someone had been there to help me when she sank her claws in. I'm glad to be able to help someone else. You didn't deserve what she did."

Especially considering what I read in the signed medical records the night before. He first went to the doctor months ago. The records didn't specify exactly what was causing his condition, only that it was something that's "not eligible" to be fixed with a little blue pill and that it "may or may not" be remedied after surgery. But it didn't say what kind of surgery. He seems healthy enough. I can't imagine what he needs surgery for.

Marc sighs somewhere behind me. "Did everyone know but me?"

"Yes," Brent and I say at the same time.

We laugh.

Brent grabs my hand, holding it loosely in his. "I'm really glad you agreed to this." His grin is dazzling. Paired with his muscular upper body, it's no wonder the guy makes women like Marissa go batshit.

"I need to finish getting ready. I'll be right out. Marc?" His eyes flick behind me and with a squeeze he drops my hand and heads back down the hallway.

"Did you want something to drink?" Marc asks.

He's standing a few feet away, hands stuffed in his pockets. Still looking to me like the most interesting man in the world. Is it weird I would rather stare at him than at the Adonis in the back?

I glance down the hall where Brent disappeared and then back to Marc. "A drink would be great. So you guys do that whole reading each other's minds thing often?"

I follow him down the hall. Everything is bright and clean. There are hardwood floors, white walls with colorful and probably original prints, and not a speck of dust to be seen.

They must have a maid service.

"Yeah. We're pretty close."

Not close enough for Brent to share what he's really going through. Maybe he's embarrassed. Or in denial. "My sisters and I do that, too. It's like I know what they're thinking before they do, and they can issue a command with no more than a look."

We stand in a kitchen full of sleek appliances and dark tile and gleaming granite countertops. My counters are ancient tiles with just as ancient grout that's a bitch to clean and riddled with stains.

I clear my throat, feeling a bit nervous at the surroundings.

He opens the fridge. "We've got beer, wine, soda, water . . ." He trails off before lifting his eyes to mine.

"A beer would be great." I need something to take the edge off.

He grabs two bottles and places them on the counter, opening a drawer to grab a bottle opener.

"Do you live nearby?" I ask.

"Brent and I both live here, actually." He pops the top off one of the beers and hands it to me.

"That's nice." The words emerge from my mouth, and I almost grimace at the lameness, but the sentiment is real. I wish I could live with one of my sisters. The city might not be quite as miserable with one of them nearby.

"He's not here much during the season, and I work a lot so . . . it just made sense, I guess. Plus, we like seeing each other." He smiles and takes a drink of his own beer.

"Did you guys always get along? My sisters and I used to fight like crazy until we got older. It wasn't until my oldest sister, Gabby, moved out that we realized we actually liked each other."

"I think that's pretty normal. Though Brent and I have always gotten along. Do your sisters live in the city?"

"I wish." I follow him into the living room. "They still live back home." The living room is mostly white and as pristine as the kitchen. There's not even a stray piece of mail left on a surface.

My tiny apartment is all clutter and dust and three-day-old dishes.

There's a sleek flat-screen TV and a bookshelf with alternating shelves of books and photos. I walk over to look at the pictures.

"Where's home?" he asks.

"Just a little town out West—is this you guys?" I pick up a framed photo of a woman with dark hair, her arms wrapped around two little boys, and she's laughing. One boy is also laughing and facing the camera—it must be

Brent, I recognize the dimples. The other boy is gazing up at her, smiling. It's obviously Marc, but there are no scars.

Marc steps up behind me. He stands to my right — so if I turn, I'll get his unscarred side?

I trail a finger over the photo. "She's beautiful."

"Thanks." His voice is soft and something in his tone catches my attention.

I rip my gaze from the photo. He's focused on the frame in my hand.

"It's my favorite picture of her. She looks so happy and, I don't know, like herself." A shadow flickers in the depths of his eyes.

My mouth pops open. "I love catching shots of people mid-laugh for that exact reason. It's just so . . . real."

His eyes meet mine and for a few very long seconds, we stare at each other.

Awareness fills the air between us, shimmering like a handful of glitter tossed into the breeze. My breath catches in my throat and my heart pounds.

"I'm ready." Brent's suddenly there in the wide doorway between the living room and the entryway. "Sorry for the wait." His smile is brief but genuine. He's wearing the same black slacks he had on earlier, with a blue sweater that brings out the color of his eyes. It's like he's stepped out of the pages of a Tommy Hilfiger catalogue, full of shiny good old-fashioned all-American looks. Like the quarterback everyone wanted in high school.

I hand the frame back to Marc and walk over to Brent, who's already grabbed my coat from the couch and holds it up for me to slip my arms inside.

"Bye, Marc." Brent heads for the door. "Don't wait up."

With one last wave at Marc, I follow Brent out the door.

Chapter Six

Photography deals exquisitely with appearances, but nothing is what it appears to be.

–Duane Michals

Gwen

Bagatelle is a French restaurant in the Meatpacking District. The cobblestone streets are surrounded by high-end clothing stores, trendy restaurants, and nightclubs. There's an elevated park built atop former railroad tracks I've taken engagement pictures in before. It's less than ten minutes from their apartment and a known celebrity haunt.

As soon as we approach the entrance, the flashes go off and questions are hurled at us through the night air.

"Hey, Brent, is this your new girlfriend?"

"Gwen, what do you think about the allegations of assault?"

Brent puts his arm around me and we hustle into the restaurant, ignoring the questions, pretending to be annoyed even though we're here to be seen.

The hostess takes us to our seat right away. The booth is near the middle—not so far from the windows the paparazzi can't see us, but far enough away to make it look like we're putting up an effort.

I can't believe any of this fools anyone. It's like a dog-and-pony show and I'm the pony. Or maybe I'm the dog.

We put in our drink orders and I glance around the space. It's very white and gold. White walls, white ceiling, white tablecloths, and gold seats on the booths. It's somewhere the glitterati go to see and be seen. It's got the kind of clientele that'll take one look at my dress and mutter to their companions, "So two seasons ago."

I take a gander at the menu and decide I'll have to order a salad. Not because I'm one of those girls that doesn't eat real food, but because that's the only thing on the menu less than twenty dollars. Unless I stick to a side dish, or maybe a dessert. It is tempting to order something from the "seafood tower" portion of the menu. For 420 dollars, those oysters better sing and dance and shower me with compliments before I eat them.

Brent leans over the table and takes my hand in his, giving me a small smile.

"I guess this is the part where we act like we're totally into each other." He pretends to consider me a moment and then grimaces. "It's going to be so difficult."

I laugh. "Flatterer."

"Totally. But I made you laugh and they're eating it up." He lifts his eyes, tilting his head toward the front window, where the paparazzi are still watching us. As yet, there's no one else entering or exiting the restaurant that they'd want to harass.

The waiter returns with our drinks and when Brent asks if I want to split the organic grass-fed truffle chicken, I agree. If he decides, he pays, right? Dammit, was that in the contract?

When we're alone again there's a moment of awkwardness and then Brent says, "Tell me about yourself."

"What? Starlee didn't already tell you everything about me?"

"Not really. Well, she sent over your whole biography, I think, but I couldn't make myself read it. It felt invasive somehow."

"It is weird. I'm sorry, I . . ." I don't know how to finish that sentence. "I'm sorry you have to do this."

"Me, too. But hey, it won't be so bad. You seem like an easy person to kick it with. I can handle this for a few weeks."

"I agree."

He's rather blasé about the whole situation, considering his job might be at risk. Not to mention his health and whatever surgery he needs to have.

I remember Marc and the circles under his eyes.

"How is Marc holding up in all this? Was he really bummed about Marissa?"

"Marc is a rock."

"He looked a little tired or something."

"He might be stressed about work, that's usually what gets him riled up, but he can handle anything."

I wonder if that's why Brent can be so carefree. Because Marc is the one who picks up all the pieces. "How long have you guys lived together?"

"I moved in before the season started. I needed a place to live." He eyes me speculatively before continuing. "The truth is that my long-time girlfriend broke up with me and I didn't want to be alone. Is it emasculating to admit that?" A flash of white teeth accompanies the deprecatory statement.

"Actually I think it's a sign of strength to admit to one's weaknesses."

Not to mention the elephant in the booth. He has one giant reason to feel emasculated, and it doesn't have anything to do with his brother.

He pretends to wipe sweat from his brow. "Phew. I'm glad that went in my favor. I am starting to wonder if it was a good idea, though. I just made Marc's life a little worse."

"You didn't hit on his girlfriend."

"No." He shakes his head. "Not at all."

"You can't control what other people do."

"I know but it's not the first time one of his girlfriends has hit on me." He frowns.

"Really?"

"Yeah. I don't understand it. It's like they're possessed. I know nearly every other man on this planet would probably chop off their left nut to be in my shoes, but it's sort of creepy how people behave when you have even a modicum of fame. I don't really know who I can trust."

"Can't trust the crazy chicken stalker."

"Right? I thought Marissa's article might get some of these people off my back. But it hasn't. And now it's affecting my job and sponsors and Marc and Dad's company." He grimaces.

"Are you worried about what will happen if this scheme doesn't work and the Sharks decide to let you go?"

"Of course I am, but I didn't do anything wrong, and the truth will come out, eventually. I didn't even think it was necessary to get you involved but Starlee was freaking out. If, worst-case scenario, this doesn't work, Marc will come up with a plan. He always does."

No wonder Starlee is so much more concerned about Brent's football career than he is. He has a backup plan. She doesn't.

Our food arrives and the topic of conversation shifts back to our more personal experiences and relationships.

Brent spears a piece of the truffle chicken with his fork. "It gets harder and harder to find someone who likes you simply because you're you and not because of your money or name. You know?"

"I do. You don't know who's real and who's not. They only like you because of your fame or what you can get them."

He nods. "Exactly. It's one of the reasons my last relationship ended. But not because she was enamored of my success. She was sure that success would lead to our downfall."

"Some people can't handle it. Too insecure." I know the feeling.

"It was hard for a while, after Bella left. Not long after that I started having health problems . . ." He trails off and his eyes flicker down to the table between us. There's definitely more to his impotence problem than what he's letting on. He clears his throat and continues. "That's when I moved in with Marc. But now I'm wondering if that was a bad idea. I don't want to drag his relationships down. It's not fair that he keeps getting caught in my crossfire."

"How many of his past relationships have . . ." I don't know how to finish that statement, but Brent knows what I'm asking.

"A few. Not as blatant as Marissa." He grimaces. "But it happened once in college, and then another time a couple years ago. It sounds weird, maybe, but I wish I knew how to stop it."

I shake my head. "Marc seems like he's a great catch. It's their loss."

"Marc's the best. He's only a few years older than me but he practically raised me after our mom died."

"I'm sorry about your mom."

He waves off my sympathy. "I was young. Marc remembers her more than I do."

We continue eating and Brent changes the subject to football. I have a few seconds to process everything we've been talking about. I totally understand where Brent is coming from; I've been on his side of the camera.

But I also get the sense that the real reason he's so blasé about all this drama is because Marc is the one who deals with the brunt of it. Marc practically raised Brent after their mom died. And when his relationship ended, he turned to Marc. And now Marc is helping him through all this drama even though he's probably going through a rough time himself.

"And now that I've talked way too much about myself, tell me more about your photography. What made you make the shift into that?"

I give him canned responses and we continue talking and conversation is easy and Brent is fun to be with. He's for sure easy on the eyes. But . . . there's no spark. When he grabs my hand as we're leaving the restaurant and the cameras are flashing, I feel nothing but kinship with him. When he kisses my cheek and opens the car door for me, it's sweet, but nothing more.

He drives me home and when I run upstairs, I'm not thinking about Brent.

I'm thinking about if I'll run into Marc when I go to the kid's center.

Chapter Seven

Beauty can be seen in all things, seeing and composing the beauty is what separates the snapshot from the photograph.
–Matt Hardy

Marc

"The website doesn't have to be anything fancy, but I definitely want to have a screen pop up that encourages donations—"

Laughter from one of the rooms stalls out my thoughts and I'm further distracted when I glance inside.

It's Gwen.

I stop and Charlie stops next to me.

Gwen's surrounded by children. She's laughing and facing away from me at an angle, camera in hand.

She's wearing jeans and a fitted, long-sleeved T-shirt topped with a colorful, soft scarf. Take the outfit by itself and it's your average autumn in New York outfit. But on Gwen . . .

The tight jeans hug her willowy figure. Her hair floats around her face, her profile aglow even from thirty feet away.

"Who are we staring at?" Charlie stage-whispers. "The blonde? Dude. She is hot."

It's Wednesday. I managed to escape the office somewhat early to head to the kids center in the Bronx. I brought Charlie with me to help set everything up. I wasn't expecting . . .

Gwen turns toward us. She's got her camera up and she catches us in her viewfinder. She moves the camera away from her face and smiles, her whole face lighting up and then she waves. "Hi!"

"Mr. Marc!" A few of the kids run over, grabbing my hands and dragging me into the room, all babbling at once.

"We're getting pictures taken."

"Am I going to be famous?"

"Do you want to have your picture taken?"

The kids are all chattering happily around us. I try to answer their questions while Charlie shakes Gwen's hand and fawns all over her.

Then one of the teenage counselors yells for them to line up to head to the gym. The whole room is chaos. I can barely make out what Charlie is saying until I'm right next to them.

"Oh, you're Brent's girlfriend?" Charlie says, disappointed. "Do you have sisters?"

"I have two sisters," Gwen answers, her tone confused.

"Okay. Two questions: are they as hot as you are and are they single?"

I tug at my tie, trying to loosen it a little. "Charlie."

Charlie rolls her eyes. "Stop being such a square."

Gwen laughs. "Both of my sisters are gorgeous. One is married with kids and the other will probably be married soon." She pats Charlie's hand. "Sorry."

Finally, the kids have gotten somewhat organized and they're heading out of the room and down the hallway. The noise level drops at least ten decibels.

"What are you doing here?" I ask Gwen.

"Starlee told me about how you guys are setting up a site for the club and I'm going to take pictures for the website. She didn't tell you?"

"No." She probably told Brent, but I haven't talked to him since he left for his away game. "This is Charlie. She's in IT at Crawford and Company."

"Oh great." Gwen turns to her. "I called over here Monday so they had time to get the parents to sign releases for the pictures. Is there is a photo size you prefer to work with? I like to keep them small so it doesn't drain the bandwidth, but you'll need at least three hundred ppi. I can pop them into Photoshop before I email them to you?"

"That's amazing," Charlie says, gazing wistfully at Gwen.

Gwen smiles at her compliment, though her eyebrows bunch together—probably since Charlie didn't actually answer the question.

I clear my throat to get their attention, but it only works on Gwen. "I'm going to show Charlie the computer room so she can get started, and then I can give you a tour of the facility and show you all the improvements we've made, along with the things that still need to be done. We can put some shots of that up on the site to encourage donors. What do you think?"

"That sounds great. I've already seen some of the building, but I haven't had a chance to get into a lot of the details. I can meet you in the gym?"

"Perfect. Come on, Charlie." I tug her arm toward the exit.

She isn't budging. "It was really nice to meet you."

"You, too."

"I'll probably see you later."

I tug again and this time she relents and starts walking backward. Slowly.

"I hope so," Gwen says.

Charlie finally turns, walking with me out the door, but not before shouting over her shoulder, "We should hang out sometime!"

When we're out of earshot, she elbows me in the side. "Dude. Since when is Brent dating *her*?"

"Since last week. Don't you pay attention to the news?"

"I read the news. No offense to your brother, but I don't read the garbage trash magazines that can't shut up about Brangelica and the Kardershians and all that other crap that doesn't mean shit to me." Her heels tap on the linoleum and cast a faint echo off the walls.

"Well, it obviously does mean shit to you since your new-girl crush is in those crap magazines with my brother."

"Huh." Her lips are pursed and I can feel her eyes on my profile. The scarred side is facing her, but that's not what she's looking at. It's probably one of the reasons I like Charlie so much. She doesn't care about my face. Doesn't even faze her. "Has Marissa met her yet?"

I pause before answering. I haven't told Charlie everything that happened. I haven't really told anyone, because it's either none of their business or they've already formed their opinions based on the media. Plus it's embarrassing. But apparently Charlie isn't kidding about not reading the tabloids. "She knows Marissa already," I finally say.

"Did Marissa try to gouge her eyes out or is she being civil?"

I frown at her. Did she know about the real Marissa, too? I must have a huge blind spot. We turn into the dark computer room and I flick on the lights. "Marissa and I are no longer dating."

"What?" she barks. "Why didn't you tell me?"

"It's a long story. And I can't really talk about it. And if you read those trash magazines, you could have already figured it out for yourself."

"Can't talk or won't talk? Marc, you know you can trust me. And you've gotta have someone to lean on sometimes. No man is an island."

"You're right, John Donne. But I'm fine." I point over at the computer parts—a few monitors, a couple slim towers, extra hard drives, and some other items I can't identify. "Here's your stuff. I'll come check on you in an hour. Don't text me if you need anything."

"This conversation isn't over, Marc!" she calls after me as I make a hasty exit.

I don't want to talk about Marissa. Or think about her. Not because it's painful or anything, but I've already moved on—a surprisingly easy endeavor.

I find Gwen in the gym on the basketball courts.

She doesn't see me at first. I sneak in the door and stand beside the counselor, who's sitting on the bleachers.

On one side of the large space, a group of kids are skipping rope, mostly older kids.

Gwen is with a group of smaller children on the opposite side, the same ones that were crowding her in the classroom. After a minute of watching, I figure they're playing some kind of freeze game. She plays a song on her phone and they all start shaking their little bodies and dancing. She stops the music at random intervals and everyone has to freeze. Whoever is still moving when she pauses the music is out of the game. They don't even get upset when Gwen points to whoever lost because they get to go stand near her, their faces bright, leaning toward her like they're little flowers and she's the sun.

They play for a few minutes. Her camera is around her neck and she takes some random shots during the game. She keeps glancing over into the corner, and after a minute I realize there's a boy standing off to the side. He's leaning against the wall and watching with his hands shoved into his pockets. He's partially hidden by a section of the bleachers, so I didn't even notice him at first.

"Come play," Gwen calls to him.

The kid on her left leans into her and says something.

"*Ven acá.*" She motions with her hand for the boy to come over. "*Te mostraré cómo jugar el juego.*"

His eyes brighten and he runs to her. She bends down to tell him something, but they're too far away for me to make out the words. After another minute, he's out boogying with the rest of the kids.

I recognize him then, a recent transfer. He doesn't speak English. Some of the other kids are bilingual but only a few, and apparently they haven't quite made friends with the new kid yet.

After the game ends and a winner is declared, the kids corral Gwen, pulling on her hands and trying to get her to dance. She relents with a laugh, passing her phone to one of the kids who had been sitting next to her, and then she's dancing with them.

I half expected someone with her height and grace to be a professional dancer. I thought she would stand up and bust out some hip-hop moves or something. Instead, she immediately acts the goofball, showing them "the sprinkler," what appears to be "the lawn mower," and then some kind of weird chicken dance that has them dissolving into giggles all around her.

When she sees me watching and laughing, she surprises me with a walk-like-an-Egyptian move straight from the eighties while sticking her tongue out and crossing her eyes. The kids erupt in fits of laughter as they try to emulate her until the music stops.

We clap and I stand, meeting her in the middle of the gym while the counselor rounds the kids up for another game.

"I didn't know you were a professional dancer, too."

"Oh yeah. I got moves. No one can 'running man' like I can."

We laugh and then the kids come over to say goodbye, hugging both of us and pulling on our hands before the counselor rounds them up again.

"Shall we?" I hold the door open for her and we leave the loud, echoing gym for the much quieter hallway.

"I didn't know you were bilingual," I say once the door shuts behind us.

"My mom's Latina. She was born in Mexico and moved here when she was eleven. She didn't speak a word of English when she got here, much like Ramon." She motions to the boy who's now laughing as he messes up the jump rope. "They didn't have anything like ESL classes back then. She's told me stories about how hard it was at first, not understanding anyone and then they expected her to take normal grade-level classes. But she learned quickly. Now she has two master's degrees and she's a college professor."

"That's amazing."

Gwen's smile is blinding. "She is amazing."

"What about your dad?"

"Ah, well that's where I get my coloring. My dad is Irish. It's funny because me and my oldest sister—Gabby—we're both like our dad, but my middle sister, Gemma, looks like my mom, all dark hair and curves and unburnable skin. I've always been so jealous of her. No one ever believes we're sisters."

"What does your dad do?" I ask.

"He used to work for the city. He's retired now, but he still plows the roads every winter and stays home and drives my mom crazy every summer. What about your dad? Brent mentioned you work for him?"

"Yep." I really have nothing nice to say about that situation, and luckily we've reached one of the rooms I wanted to show her. "This is the music room." I open a side door and click on the light. "We funded the purchase of all of the instruments, and there's an orchestra teacher that comes in once a week and teaches some of the older kids the strings."

"That's so cool."

"It is."

She snaps a few photos and then shoots me a sidelong glance. "Can I get a picture of you over there by the cello?"

"Oh no. I don't do the whole picture thing."

She pouts. "Please? Shots with people are so much more interesting. And I'm sure people who donate want to see the man behind the charity."

"I'm not the man behind anything."

"That's not what Brent told me the other night."

"You guys talked about me on your date?"

She glances around the empty room, as if paparazzi are hiding under one of the teeny tiny desks. "You know it wasn't a real date."

"Either way, it seemed to work."

She nods. "It did."

There were some tweets from *TZM* and an article in *Page Seven* the very next morning. "That's good. Brent doesn't deserve this kind of backlash."

"I'm sure it will blow over soon. People with half a brain will realize she's doing it for the publicity and personal gain."

"I hope you're right. It's crazy how he just wants to play a little ball, but it comes along with all this other crap."

I nod. "We talked about that. And I can completely relate. Well, sort of. I've never been named the world's sexiest anything." She flashes me a wink. "But I modeled for a few years. In any industry where you're subject to public scrutiny, it's always about optics. Appearances are more important than reality. It's why I wanted to leave. It has a way of wearing you down, you know? And I wanted to do something more than base all my dreams on my face because eventually those looks will be gone and you can't base your entire self-worth on that."

"Is that why you got into photography?"

"One of the many reasons. I enjoyed modeling—minus the drama and politics—but I want to make more of a difference. You know? Like what you guys are doing here."

"It's nothing. Our mom started the funding for this place. I've just kept it up."

She takes a few more pictures and I watch her. We're silent, but it's not uncomfortable. She's focused on her shots, crouching down in a few places before standing up.

When she's finished, we exit the room and I lead her farther down the hall, pointing out the walls we've repaired and painted, the floors that have been redone, and also the things that still need work like the chipped plaster and the leaky AC units.

My phone keeps ringing—people from the office calling—but I cancel the calls and eventually put my phone on silent. Everyone relies on me too much.

As we walk I try to keep Gwen on my good side, the uninjured side, but somehow she keeps drifting to the scarred side again. I can feel her eyes on me as we traverse the school, no matter how many times I point out the kids' quiet room, a lending library, a freaking water fountain, *anything* to get her spotlight off me. I didn't have this concern with Charlie, but that was different. I care more about what Gwen thinks of me.

"Can I ask you something kind of personal?" She stops in the middle of the hall, and I stop next to her. "You don't have to answer," she adds.

I nod. "Go ahead." Here it comes—the scar talk.

"What happened to your mom?"

Or not. I take a breath before answering. "Heart failure. One moment she was fine, the next she was gone."

"I'm so sorry. It sounds like she was a wonderful person."

"Yeah, she was a great mom. We wouldn't be the same without her. We grew up in a middle-class neighborhood upstate when we could have afforded a penthouse in the city. But that's not what she wanted for us."

"That's smart. You appreciate things more when they aren't so readily available."

I nod. "She was raised in a middle-class family, and she wanted us to have a normal childhood. I think because of our dad."

"He had a different childhood?"

"Our grandfather started the company when he was eighteen and built it from the ground up. It started as a small supplier of specialized items for restaurants, and then he kept adding and expanding until it became a huge empire. Dad took it over when grandpa died. It was already a success though, so he basically just had to maintain everything. It made him perceive things differently, but I think that's why he loved our mom so much. She never cared about the money and she was the only person he let affect him at all."

She nods and opens her mouth to speak, but then closes it again.

I can't believe I even shared that much with her. We barely know each other, but there's something about her. Something beyond the blonde hair and fresh-faced good looks.

Perhaps sensing my reluctance, she changes the subject. "What's in here?" She peeks into an empty room.

"Ah, this is a good one. The art room." I open the door and flick on the light to reveal the mural on the opposite wall. A couple of the older kids are handy with the spray paint cans—something I don't want to think about too closely.

One of the windows was left open to air out the smell, letting in a cool fall breeze.

The wall is covered in a mishmash of various pieces. There are different faces, brightly painted flowers, musical notes, and instruments. There's a random bunny with giant teeth in the opposite corner, a painting of a half-peeled banana, and other smaller items, all squeezed into the space, a collage of bright oddities. The amazing part is the intricacy of each piece. Although none of them really make sense, they all fit together like they're meant to be here.

"This is amazing." Gwen snaps a few pictures. "Who did this?"

"A couple of the older boys. Jake and Marcellus. They're both very talented. This is an attempt for them to showcase their art in a way that doesn't involve the destruction of property."

I move closer to the piece, smiling as I remember helping the boys paint the base coat. When I had to stop and take a break because my back hurt, they kept calling me "old man."

The snap of the shutter nearby startles me.

Gwen is standing next to me, camera in hand, closer than I realized.

"Sorry." She smiles, sheepish. "I told you I wanted to take your picture."

"No, I'm sorry. Because no doubt your camera is now broken."

She chuckles and rolls her eyes before putting a hand on my arm. "Stop with the self-deprecating comments already. You're a handsome guy."

"Maybe once upon a time."

She's standing so close I can see the darker flecks of blue in her eyes. The world stops, the moment inflating between us like a slowly expanding balloon. When will it pop?

She reaches up and I suck in air with an audible hiss as her hand feathers over my face. The scarred side.

Then I forget to breathe completely as her fingers smooth over my cheek, just a whisper of a touch, before her hand drops to her side. "What happened?"

I gather my wits and remember to breathe. "Shark attack."

Her brows lift. "Really?"

"No."

She laughs. "You don't have to tell me. I'm very nosy today."

"It's no big deal. I've always wished I had a cool story but the reality is that it was a snowboarding accident when I was a teenager. And before you ask, I've talked to professionals about getting it fixed and it's not worth it since it's right around the eye area. Too risky."

She tilts her head at me, her lips purse a little. "I wasn't going to ask that. Why would you need to get it fixed? I told you, chicks dig scars."

I laugh. "That hasn't been my experience."

"I find that hard to believe."

"Believe it."

We're silent for another long moment, considering each other.

Then she speaks. "Do you want to get some food?"

Chapter Eight

The beauty of the past belongs to the past.
–Margaret Bourke-White

Gwen

Marc's eyes widen when I ask him if he wants food.

"Not like a date," I rush to assure him. "After all, I'm with your brother. Or sort of with your brother. Well, not at all with your brother but you know that. I just thought, you know, you might like to eat." The laugh that emerges from my mouth is awkward and nervous to my own ears.

What is wrong with me? You'd think I haven't talked to a real live person before.

He must not notice, though, because he nods. "I haven't eaten since breakfast. Let's go see if Charlie wants anything."

We walk back to the computer room, where we find the tiny redhead clicking keys on a laptop and muttering to herself.

"Hey, Charlie. You want food?"

"You guys go ahead." She waves, her eyes never leaving the screen in front of her and her fingers still tapping away. "There's some issues with the basic infrastructure of their server and I want to make sure their LAN can handle the load when we get hella people to donate."

"Right. You can call for a company car to take you home when you're done."

"Got it." She flicks a thumb up, then keeps typing.

Marc calls somewhere for a car to come get us as we walk to the front entrance. We stop in at the office to say goodbye to the director and let her know that Charlie is still there working. The director gives Marc a big hug before we exit for the streets.

Within minutes, a sleek sedan is pulling up and Marc opens the door for me to slide in.

"This is fancy," I say.

"Welcome to the lifestyles of the rich and not so famous."

I laugh. "I'm more used to the lifestyles of the broke and desperate."

He watches me in the dim interior of the car, broken by the occasional flash of a street lamp as we drive. "Not anymore, right?"

"Well. Not quite that bad. There was a time, though, when I had given up the modeling jobs and I wasn't getting nearly enough photography shoots. Let's just say if it weren't for Maria at the bodega on the corner, I might have starved."

He laughs and then his head tilts a little as he regards me. "You're not like most people I've met."

I grimace. "Is that a bad thing?"

"No, it's a refreshing thing. Most people don't talk about their hard times, you know? Everyone has a façade they like to present to the world, and it's all the best and happiest moments."

I shrug. "I don't know. I don't see the point in trying to be someone other than myself. I tried that. Didn't work out."

He nods, his eyes assessing me for a moment before he glances away. "What do you like to eat?"

"I'm not picky. I'll eat anything that won't eat me first."

"Have ever you had a burger from Raoul's?"

My mouth drops open. "What? No. They only make like twelve of them a night. It's damn near impossible to get one."

He smiles slowly. "What if I told you that everything you think you know is a lie?"

"Well, I'd say hand me a red pill, Morpheus."

He laughs. "You know, he never actually says that line in the movie."

"I know. Yet another falsehood spread by viral memes." I shake my head in mock outrage. "What is this world coming to?"

We laugh together and then I have to ask, trying not to get too excited, "Can you really get us burgers from Raoul's?"

"We supply all of their cooking equipment. So yes. I don't typically call in these types of favors, but I'd be willing to make an exception for the woman who's saving my brother. Although I have to admit I'm surprised you'll eat one."

"Why is that surprising?"

"Most models I've been around only consume cigarettes and diet soda with a splash of cocaine."

I grin. "Well there's your mistake. I'm not a model."

He calls in our order from the car and the driver takes us to SoHo. We're dropped off in front of the small storefront and when we walk in, they immediately seat us at the bar. The bartender greets Marc and they shake hands.

Marc introduces me as a friend and then we order drinks. Once we each have a glass of beer in front of us, the bartender goes to the back to get our food.

Raoul's is an artsy French bistro with three dining rooms. The walls are decorated with nudes and jazz portraits. Above us spans a tin ceiling. The space is filled with the scent of garlic and fresh baked bread. It's not quite five yet, but people already fill the tables and crowd one end of the bar.

"You didn't introduce me as Brent's girlfriend."

He shrugs out of his suit jacket and hangs it on the seat. "Should I have?"

"Well, we wouldn't want people to get the wrong idea."

"I don't think we have to worry about that."

I open my mouth to argue with him, but then the bartender brings us our plates and for a second I forget my own name because the mouthwatering burger in front of me looks like a work of art. It's a giant brisket patty topped with greens and piquant au poivre sauce inside a challah bun. "Oh, wow."

"I know."

There's a comfortable silence for a few minutes, amongst the tinkling of silverware against plates and the murmur of the early dinner crowd, while we eat our burgers.

"Can I ask you a question?" he asks.

"Considering the third degree I subjected you to all afternoon?" I pretend to think about it. "Nah, you get nothing."

"Seems fair."

I take a sip of beer and then wink at him. "Go ahead. I probably owe you one or twelve."

"Why did you agree to date Brent?"

"A few reasons," I hedge. It feels wrong admitting I did it to further my own career. Of course, that wasn't the only reason, but it was the main one.

"I guess I'm surprised you aren't already in a relationship or dating someone else, is all."

"I'm not really looking for anything like that right now. I don't have time for a relationship. I've been working really hard on a project and if everything goes as planned, I'll be traveling a lot and it's not fair to start something that will turn into long distance at best and end in a fiery pile of pain at worst. So this arrangement with Brent works out for me. Since it's temporary."

"So what you're telling me is that you're a romantic."

"Is it that obvious?"

We share a smile at our mutual sarcasm.

"Travelling sounds fun," he says. "I've always wanted to take a year and just travel the world with a backpack and no firm plans. Just leave everything behind and go where the wind takes me."

"That does sound fun. Sounds like we share a bit of the wanderlust."

We turn back to our burgers in silence for a few moments before Marc speaks again. "But what if you fall in love?"

I nearly choke on my bite of delicious beef. "You think I'm going to fall in love with your brother?"

He shrugs. "It happens a lot."

"People don't fall in love with Brent. They're fans that are in lust and they fall in love with the idea of him."

"Maybe. So you think you're immune?"

"I do." At his disbelieving expression, I continue, "What? You want me to fall in love with him?"

"I want Brent to be happy. The rest of it doesn't really matter. It would make a nice story, though, don't you think? Two people, pretending to date and then they fall in love and live happily ever after? I feel like I've seen that movie a few times."

"This isn't the movies."

Except it starts to feel unreal because a familiar face enters the restaurant behind Marc. And like in the movies he just mentioned—except it's more of a horror story—my vision narrows and my throat constricts as if I'm being choked by an invisible hand.

"Gwen, you okay?" Marc's voice is coming from far away.

Lucky catches me staring and then everything around us slows down to a crawl as he acknowledges my gaze with a small smirk. Then he heads in our direction.

Oh, no.

"Gwen, darling," he says. He air kisses me on both cheeks, his hands gripping my shoulders briefly before he steps back and smiles at us, all charm and grace as if the last time I saw him he hadn't been a cheating, phony, no-good piece of rat dung.

He looks the same. Too thin. Too chiseled. Too perfectly put together in an expensive shirt and distressed pants that he pays extra for to look casual and like he's not trying too hard.

I'm speechless. Terrified. There's a lump in my throat and I can't speak around it.

Marc thankfully steps into the breech. "I'm Marc Crawford," he says, shaking Lucky's hand.

Through the pounding of my heart in my ears, they exchange names and pleasantries.

And then I see her. My former best friend is at the door, eyes pointed down toward the phone in her hand, looking bored and beautiful with her dark wavy hair, designer clothes, and flawless face.

Becca.

She was the first friend I made in New York. And then she ripped my heart in two.

83

I try not to hold hate in my heart, but all I can think when I look at her is I hope she gets a high five. In the face. With a van. A big one.

Lucky is speaking to me and I rip my eyes away from Becca. "I saw the news about you and the footballer," he says, like he's fucking British or something. "*Lucky* thing, snagging that fish. Maybe you'll be able to use his connections to help fix your . . . problems."

He's always using his name with double meaning. I never realized how lame it was until he was gone. He would always say, *they call me Lucky, because I am Lucky and because I get Lucky.* In hindsight, it's so stupid I don't know why I ever thought he was an interesting person.

But now that he's here in front of me, everything I've thought about saying to him if I ever saw him again is stuck in my throat. About how my only problem was not recognizing him for the snake that he is before it was too late. About how I trusted him and he treated me like trash.

But once again, Marc interjects, his tone firm. "We're the ones who are lucky. My family and I support her one hundred percent and we would never let anyone hurt her."

Lucky has enough of a survival instinct to step back. He's not the biggest fish in this pond. "Nice to see you again, Gwennie. We have to get together and catch up soon."

He was the only one who ever called me Gwennie, something I used to think was cute but now makes me want to puke my burger all over him.

I still haven't said anything. I'm barely breathing. Lucky walks away into the other room, and Becca follows without so much as a glance in my direction.

Somehow Marc manages to get our food bagged up and a few minutes later, he's ushering me outside and into the car. The sedan moves smoothly down the street and Marc gives me a couple of minutes to gather myself before he speaks.

I'm grateful for the momentary peace. It's like he knows exactly what I need.

But then, of course, he has to ask. "Who was that bonehead?"

I've been gazing out the window, shell-shocked. But now I force my gaze to meet Marc's. "Lucky Carter."

"Is that supposed to mean something to me?"

"He's a model. He's well known in that crowd. I used to . . . date him." At least, I thought we were a couple.

He thought we were casually boning while he also casually boned every other female within a ten-mile radius, including my "friend" Becca. But I don't want to tell Marc about how clueless I was. How everyone laughed at me behind my back when I would gush about my "boyfriend."

I was so stupid.

Seeing Lucky brings all those insecurities rushing to the surface.

But then I glance over at Marc and feel an equal rush of appreciation. He stood up for me. No one has done that in so long.

"You know, it doesn't matter what you look like on the outside. Whether you're scarred," I reach up and cup his injured cheek, "or beautiful. We all have them. But some scars are invisible."

I drop my hand and turn back to the window, watching the city lights rush by.

A few minutes later, Marc shifts in the seat next to me, watching me. "I was a pretty good snowboarder."

"Yeah?"

"I qualified for nationals when I was sixteen."

"Brent isn't the only one in the family with athletic ability."

He nods his head once, a slight dip downward. "But ever since the accident, I haven't so much as touched a board. I can barely look at one."

"What happened?"

"I was an idiot. There had been a big storm and then a major freeze and the snow was slick. I was young, reckless, thought I was invincible. I crashed. Ran into a tree. There were icicles, and they fell on me. My goggles were askew from the collision. This side was exposed." He fingers the damaged side of his face.

He puts his hand back down on the seat between us.

After a few long seconds I cover it with my own.

His palm turns into mine and the movement makes our fingers link. The gesture is so natural, his hand warm and steady against my own, it just feels . . . right. Like we've held hands a hundred times before.

The steady pressure and heat of his fingers are a comfort I didn't know I needed.

I wonder if my hand is having the same effect on him, but I don't ask. Words might ruin it. We make the rest of the drive to my apartment in silence.

Chapter Nine

It is more important to click with people
than to click the shutter.
  –Alfred Eisenstaedt

Gwen

"Gwen." The voicemail is from my sister, Gemma. Her voice is clipped and serious. *"I saw on the news you're dating some freaking football player? What the hell! If you don't call me back within twenty-four hours, I'm calling the authorities. Don't test me."*

"She has guns," Sam calls out in the background right before the click.

That's the fourth message I've gotten on my cell phone since Wednesday. It's been three days since my date with Marc that wasn't really a date at all.

But it felt like one. It felt like more of a date than the lunch with Brent yesterday.

We had to get together at least once while he was in town and not busy with training. Brent held my hand. We talked and laughed while pictures and videos were taken by an entertainment channel. He even kissed me. On the lips, mouths shut.

And yet, the simple, quiet moment with Marc in the car felt a million times more . . . *more*.

His hand in mine, so reassuring, so real.

Hell, exchanging silly texts over the last few days has felt a million times more, and I can't even see or hear him.

I've been avoiding returning Gemma's call because I have to lie to her. I can't tell her the truth about Brent. The thought of lying to my family makes my stomach hurt.

Instead, earlier in the week, I scratched out a few minutes in between shoots to call Starlee and let her know how Marc and I ran into Lucky at Raoul's. I had to let her know about the potential fallout. I wasn't going to let Lucky use me for publicity ever again.

"It's fine," she said with a laugh. "No one will think anything is happening with you and Marc."

"Why wouldn't they?"

"Marc's great, but he's not Brent."

The comment made want to reach through the phone and strangle her. But I said nothing, even though in my mind the reverse is true. Brent's great, but he's not Marc.

And I can't keep avoiding Gemma. I call her and Sam one night after I get home.

She answers on the first ring and immediately begins interrogating me about Brent.

I can't tell her the truth, even though I want to. But I signed that agreement. I can trust Gemma, but she'll tell Sam. And Sam is also trustworthy, but he has a giant "trustworthy" family that would no doubt be apprised of the situation as well. The fewer people who know, the better and the less likely it will be that someone will accidentally say the wrong thing to the wrong person.

I should have known my family would find out eventually, but they don't normally stay on top of things like the New York scene.

"We had an agreement," Gemma says. "You aren't allowed to date anyone before I meet them first. If I had met *he who shall not be named* before it got serious, I could have warned you away from him. Or throat punched him or something."

"I know, Gemma, but it's not like that. We've only gone on a couple dates. It's nothing serious."

"I want to meet the new guy, too," Sam calls from somewhere near Gemma. There's a shuffle and then he's on the phone. "Can I meet him?"

"Uhhhh," I stall.

"I promise I won't be weird. Can I bring a rookie card? Do you think he'll sign it? How do you think he'd feel about extremely long hugs from his potential future brother-in-law?"

There's more shuffling and Gemma murmuring, "Dude, they're not getting married. Stop it. No, I'm sure he does not hang out with Eli Manning. Anyway," she says into the phone. "I would like to come and see you to make sure everything is okay."

"Gemma, it's fine. He's nothing like Lucky. Trust me."

After the whole Lucky debacle and subsequent meltdown, Gemma flew out to New York. She kind of had to. I didn't contact anyone for nearly a month. I went through a phase where I didn't work, I just lay in my apartment watching *Bridget Jones's Diary* and listening to Taylor Swift's "White Horse" over and over again.

When Gemma found me, I was in bad shape. I had slid into a severe depression. I wasn't showering or doing much of anything except ordering takeout and crying. She cleaned me up, made me eat better food and go outside. She brought me out of the darkness. Hence the overprotective bit. I know it's just because she loves me.

She doesn't want me to go through that again. I don't blame her; I don't want to go through that again either.

Gemma and Sam even paid my rent a couple months in advance until I could get back on my feet, something I've been repaying a little each month ever since.

"Are you sure? Because I heard there was some chick who said he assaulted her."

"How are you hearing these things?"

"I have friends."

"One of Lucy's friends told us," Sam calls out.

"Well it's not true. It was Marissa. She's the one who wrote the article about me last year. She's full of it."

She silent for a few long seconds. "So you're sure there's nothing serious happening with this Brent Crawford guy?"

Sam's voice calls in the background. "I wouldn't call a nearly thousand-yard season his first year nothing serious!"

"I don't even know what that means," Gemma tells him.

"Everything's going to be fine. I promise," I say with a sigh.

"I want to see this guy. Sam, where's my computer?"

She and Sam mutter to each other and I think I hear a kiss before she comes back on the line.

They're so cute it's disgusting.

Gemma and Sam have been together for almost two years now. We grew up next door to Sam and his family. We've known them forever.

Keys tap in the background and then Gemma says, "You're right. He's nothing like Lucky or those other waifish weirdos you modeled with. He is hot." She gasps and there's more clicking. "Look at those biceps."

"I'd totally date him," Sam says.

"Yeah, he's good-looking," I say, "But—"

There's a buzz at my door.

"Hold on, someone's here."

"Don't answer, it might be a mugger."

"Muggers don't ring the bell."

"But you're in a big city. Maybe it's a serial killer. They ring bells all the time, you know. They're smarter than your average criminal."

"Not everyone in New York is a criminal."

"So you say, but I've watched *Law & Order*, I know the truth."

I push the button. "Yeah?"

"Is this Gwen McDougall?"

It's a female voice with a Southern accent.

I release the button. That can only be one person.

"What?" Gemma asks in my ear.

"It's a girl I met the other night."

"What does she want?"

"How am I supposed to know?"

"Um, I don't know, why don't you ask her?"

I hit the intercom. "Hi, Scarlett?"

"Oh, hi!" Her voice over the speaker is a combination of surprised and excited. "You know it's me!" There's a pause and her voice drops an octave. "How did you know it was me?"

"Your accent sort of gives you away." Plus it's not like I have girlfriends coming over all the time. Or ever.

"Oh, right. I brought you some cupcakes just like I said I would."

"Um. Hold on." I put my phone back to my ear. "She brought me cupcakes. Is that weird?"

"What? No. Southern people bringing baked goods are always welcome. Let her in."

I hesitate and Gemma immediately calls me on it.

"Dude. You're always whining about not having any friends in the city and blah blah blah. Why are you being a weirdo?"

"Would you quit pointing out my own hypocrisy? You're my sister. You're supposed to enable my delusions."

"Not everyone is Becca. Why don't you let someone surprise you?"

"Ugh, fine." I push the intercom. "Come on up, Scarlett." I click the button that will unlock the door. "If she comes up here and murders me, I'm blaming you," I tell Gemma.

"If you can't protect yourself against some chick with cupcakes, that's your own problem. You're always saying everyone judges you based on your looks. Maybe they're not the problem."

"Do you always have to be so honest?"

"Yes."

There's a tentative knock at the door.

"I gotta go, I'll call you tomorrow."

"Unless you've died from cupcakes and hospitality."

"Haha."

We hang up and I answer the door.

Scarlett's standing there with a bright smile and a plate full of baked goods. She wasn't kidding the other night when she walked me to my front door.

"Hi. Thanks for bringing those. Come on in." I hold the door open, but instead of coming in, she just stands there.

The smile slowly melts from her face and then she bursts into tears.

"Well, shit." I grab her free arm and tug her gently inside before the wailing disturbs the neighbors.

I don't know what to do.

"Are you okay?" I'm not even sure what she's crying about.

We're standing in the small entryway, one sobbing redhead and one clueless blonde. This sounds like it needs a punch line. Her plate is drooping forward as she cries, her eyes shut, forehead wrinkled.

I grab the cupcakes before they end up in a red velvet soufflé on the floor.

"He said it was," she sniffs and sobs, "*uninspired.*"

I lead her to the living room, pushing her gently down onto the futon and shoving some tissues in her hand. "Who said what now?" I sit next to her.

"The guy at the thing. He said my cooking was . . . was unsophisticated." She sniffs and wipes at her nose with the tissues.

"Okaaay. The guy at the thing." I peel the plastic wrap off the plate still in my hands, pulling out a white-frosting-topped cupcake. "Looks pretty inspired to me." I take a giant bite and immediately moan as the sweet, delicate flavor explodes in my mouth. "Oh, wow. This is really good." The words are garbled since I'm chewing. I swallow. "These are definitely the best cupcakes I've ever had."

I'm not even lying. They're really good. Moist, sweet, but not too sweet, just like I like them.

Her cries have mellowed down into sniffles. "You really think so?"

"Absolutely. Here, try." I shove the plate in her direction.

She takes a small bite and then nods. "It *is* good."

"So this guy at the thing is full of shit."

She lets out a sniff-laugh combo. "He's not just the guy at the thing. He's *Guy* Chapman."

I purse my lips. I know that name. "Is that the chef guy who's always yelling at everyone?"

"No. That's a different famous chef. Guy is the brooding handsome one who doesn't have to say much of anything to make people run crying." She flaps a hand. "Apparently."

"Oh, right. I think I've eaten at a couple of his restaurants. Yeah, he's hot. Smoldery. Lethal combination. Well, if he made you cry, he sucks. And I've never understood the name Guy, it's like naming someone Dude or Chick or Bro. It doesn't make sense." I nudge her with an elbow. "You should tell him that."

"Y'all can tell him yourself because I'm not telling him anything. I had an interview for his new restaurant, a specialty dessert shop, and I blew it." She sighs and wipes her nose again.

"I'm sure it wasn't as bad as you think it was."

She laughs and it turns into another sob. "I sort of . . . set him on fire."

"How did you manage that?"

"I was putting the finishing touches on a crème brûlée, and I tripped."

"You tripped? With one of those little mini torches?"

She grimaces and then nods. "I tripped into him. I didn't actually set him completely on fire, that was a slight exaggeration. I kind of burned his chef's jacket."

"Oh."

"His lucky chef's jacket."

"Oh, no."

"Oh, yes. And he's known to be a bit of a perfectionist." She blows her nose into the napkins I handed her. "I'm like the antithesis of perfection. Everything I touch gets ruined."

I consider her for a minute and think about what Gemma said, and my life, and how I've held everyone at a distance for the last year while internally complaining about how terrible the city is and wanting to run away from everything. Is Gemma right? Am I the problem? I take a breath. "You know what would go great with these cupcakes?"

"What?"

"Tequila."

~*~

So tequila and cupcakes are actually terrible together. But an hour later, we've put the tequila back in the cupboard and had a couple glasses of wine and three cupcakes each.

"You got the interview for the job because of the article about us?"

I'm not the only one who had some life changes after Liz ran the Wonder Woman article.

"Pretty much." Scarlett puts her empty wine glass on the table in front of us. "When I went to check on the status of my application, the producer recognized me from the picture and put my name at the top of the list. Then I blew it."

"I'm sure you'll find a better job, eventually."

"I don't want a job. I'm already working as a short order cook at one of those all-night diners that has the best coffee in the world and I have to wear a polyester blend shirt and the most unflattering pants known to man. I want a career. I want to have my own kitchen where I can make the menu and tell people what to do. This was a chance to have all of that."

"I know the feeling. There will be other opportunities for you, I'm sure of it."

She pats me on the shoulder. "But things are going good for you, right? I saw an article with you and that football guy." She whistles. "He's a real looker. My granny would call him a prime pickle. "

I purse my lips and nod, considering Granny's newest phrase. "Why a pickle?"

"I think it's a euphemism for something else. Granny is a bit of a horndog."

I snort out a laugh. "I guess so."

"So have you had a look at his pickle?"

"Um. No."

"Well why not?"

I can't tell her about Brent, for obvious legal reasons, but can I talk to her about Marc? No. I can't. Nothing will ever come of it. I can't have a relationship with anyone, let alone the brother of the guy I'm fake dating. And I can't mention the fake dating, so if I try to explain it out loud without that important little tidbit, it'll sound more like cheating.

So I settle for a slight untruth. "We're taking it slow. He's a gentleman."

She sighs. "I didn't know those existed anymore."

"Well when you find all your dates on Grindr, I'm sure it seems that way. But I'm sure there will be more opportunities for you as well. For a career and for a man."

"Maybe. Or I'll have to move back to Blue Falls. I don't want to go back, though. I can't go back. There's nothing for me there."

"No restaurants in Blue Falls, Texas?"

"There's two eateries in town, a diner and a more upscale restaurant, but they're both owned by the same man and, well, suffice it to say I dated him and it didn't end well. Story of my life."

I take a sip of wine and refill her glass. "What happened there?"

She shakes her head, a slight flush crawling up her neck. It must have been bad. "You do not want to know. The only thing that might compel me to return is my little sister, Reese. She just started college this year."

We talk for a while about our families and she tells me more about Reese. I tell her about my sisters, too, and by the time the clock strikes midnight, I'm tired but happy.

I haven't had a night where I could sit and talk to someone like this in forever. Even though I can't share all the drama or the truth about my relationship with Brent, it's still . . . nice.

We agree to have drinks at some point over the next week and by the time the Uber shows up and I lock the front door behind Scarlett, a bubble of hope has formed in my chest.

I forgot how much I enjoy just hanging out and talking with a friend. Gossiping about boys and family and life . . . I've been so good at pushing people away for the last year I didn't realize how much I was holding back who I am and what I've been missing out on.

Maybe New York isn't so bad after all.

Chapter Ten

Work is something you can count on, a
trusted, lifelong friend who never deserts you.
—Margaret Bourke-White

Marc

I spend a couple of days immersed in work, attempting to forget about Marissa and everything that happened.

Not my own heartbreak—my heart is surprisingly okay with Marissa being out of the picture. But the fallout for Brent is making my blood pressure rise. Dad's on me to "fix it" since Brent is the star behind all of our proposals to investors for the store expansion. The bad press is affecting the company. Heaven forbid Dad worry about his children's emotions instead of the bottom line.

On top of that, football has been Brent's dream since we were kids. It's not fair, it's not right that a woman I picked to date holds his future in her lying, manipulative hands. This fake-relationship idea needs to work. The guilt is wearing on me. Guilt that only grows when I think about Gwen.

Her fingers in mine, and more importantly, her fingers on my face. Twice.

Twice she's touched me. On purpose. Women don't do that. Every single person I've dated since the accident went out of her way to avoid it.

Then I remember running into her ex—Mr. Cheekbones—and the way he stole the light from her eyes. You don't really think about beautiful people having relationship problems, but that doesn't make sense, I guess. Everyone has problems sometimes. Looks have nothing to do with it.

Some scars are invisible.

She's an odd but irresistible combination of maturity and innocence.

Brent went to lunch with her the other day and I avoided all publicity of them canoodling for the cameras.

Since our little run-in at the kids club, we've emailed back and forth about the website a few times. She sent me the pictures she took; I sent her a thank you.

Then today she sent me a *Matrix* meme with Morpheus saying, *What if I told you to have a nice day?*

It made me smile and I want to return the favor, so a bit later I return the email with one of Keanu Reeves—less Neo, more *Bill and Ted's Excellent Adventure*. The meme has a goofy shot of Keanu with his mouth half open and it reads, *What if soy milk is just regular milk introducing itself in Spanish?*

An hour later, I get a grumpy cat meme. *I purred once. It was awful.*

Laughing, I immediately put aside my reports and start googling for memes.

I send one back to her of Chuck Norris: *When Chuck Norris left for college, he told his father, "You're the man of the house now."*

When I turn back to my reports, I'm still smiling.

A few minutes later, my inbox dings with a black and white picture of Chewbacca. *Uuur Arrr Uhhhr Ahhhr Aaarhg.*

I laugh and type back, *You win.*

After that, every time my inbox dings, I jump to check it, but it's always from someone in the company about invoices and interagency memos and work things. Doesn't stop my heart from leaping every time.

Eventually, she writes back and I'm smiling before I even open the email.

Yes! I've always wanted to win a meme war. Now that all my dreams have been actualized, I can quit this photo shoot and pursue meme challenging full time. Or maybe make it home before nine for the first time all week. Did Charlie need anything else for the website? I haven't heard from her.

Not wanting to come off as too eager, I wait a little bit before responding. Plus I am actually busy, although the more I get to know Gwen, the more dangerous I realize she is. If she asked me to drop everything I'm doing right now, I would likely sprint out the door.

The question at the end throws me a little. Why send me a message and not Charlie directly? Did she ask the question to keep our little message chain going?

No.

I'm reading too much into it.

I haven't heard any complaints from Charlie, but I think she's enamored of you. I cede the meme championship to you. You are a worthy competitor. Before nine sounds like a dream. I'll be lucky to make it out of here before sunrise. I'll renew the challenge of the memes if I do, so you better get you're A game on. I was being easy on you before.

I add a winky face.

Are winking faces creepy?

I delete it.

Should I ask her something so that she responds? My mind blanks. What could I ask her about? Everything I think up sounds way too cheesy.

In the end I leave it as is and hit send.

Time passes. I put out fires and try not to watch my inbox too closely.

It's dark outside when Dad stops by my office on his way out. "Did you get the scheduling done for the guys from Tokyo?"

"I'm on it." Like always. "Are you going to be around for Thanksgiving? Brent and I are driving up to the Hamiltons'. They invited you as well."

But I know what he's going to say. We go through this every year. "Can't go this time. I'm taking Glory to Saint Bart's."

Glory must be the newest fling. I'll be surprised if she makes it to Thanksgiving; it's over a week away.

I try to ignore the twinge of disappointment that hits me. It's not even that I want to hang out with Dad. Most of the time, I'd rather go for a root canal than deal with him at the office. But he's my father. You'd think he'd at least extend an invitation for us to join him. He has no idea that I'd break my right arm for the chance to travel anywhere beyond the Eastern Seaboard.

Besides, maybe he'd be different away from here. Maybe it would be more like it was before Mom died.

I should be used to his rejection by now, but endless repetition of the same stab doesn't stop the sting.

"That's fine," I bite out. "Will you at least tell Brent what you're doing so I don't have to?"

"Brent won't care. He's a grown man." Like I'm not. "Besides, you'll see him before I do."

"Right."

"Don't be running your guilt trips on me, boy. You're worse than your mother."

"I don't see that as an insult."

There's a tap on my door right before it swings open. "Hey, Marc, I brought you some—oh I'm so sorry to interrupt."

It's Gwen. She's wearing black yoga pants that hug her curves and a soft pink long-sleeved top, and her hair is pulled back in a messy ponytail. There isn't so much as a hint of makeup on her face, but she's still the most beautiful woman I've ever seen and my heart starts beating triple time. She's holding a brown paper shopping bag.

"You aren't interrupting anything, darling," Dad flirts. "Who have we got here?"

"I'm Gwen." She reaches out her free hand and Dad takes it in both of his. He shakes it—and doesn't let go.

"You're here to see Marc." There's an unspoken question mark on the end of that sentence. He might as well have said, Why is someone like *you* coming to see someone like *him*?

She flushes a little while yanking her hand away. "Well, yeah, I brought him some food because he said he'd be here late but I'm, uh, Brent's girlfriend."

"Of course you are. A beautiful woman like you wouldn't be with this blender face." Dad laughs.

I sigh and avert my eyes. The papers on my desk are suddenly *fascinating*. For the first time in the longest time, shame wraps its warm fingers around my neck like a scarf. I thought I'd become accustomed to his comments, but in front of Gwen they pack an extra punch.

"I think any woman with a modicum of intelligence would be proud to be with someone as smart and talented as Marc." Her voice is like steel wrapped in candy, both sweet and sharp.

Surprised, I lift my eyes and see Gwen staring my father down, her eyes bright, her face flushed.

She's defending me. With a smile.

And dad would never dare to gainsay a woman as beautiful as Gwen.

"Touché, my dear." He chuckles. "It was nice meeting you. Tell Brent I said hello when you see him and to watch out because I might be stealing his girl." He laughs again and pats her on the shoulder as he leaves my office.

"Well." Gwen walks over and puts her bag on my desk. "He's interesting."

"That's one word for it."

"I brought something to ease your sorrows." She pulls out a couple of containers.

"Is the cure to my father's irrational behavior in that bag?"

"No, but it might be the cure to not caring about your father's irrational behavior." She smiles gamely and pops off the lid to show me. "Red velvet cupcakes. Made by a true Southerner. You have to try one." She holds it out toward me. "I brought real food, too, but I've always thought it makes sense to start with dessert."

I take a bite and chew. "Wow. These are great. Where did you get them?"

She pauses for a second and then says, "A friend of mine. Her name is Scarlett. She's a chef."

"You came all the way here to bring me food?"

"If I didn't, I would be sitting at home eating them by myself and you and Brent could use the calories more than me. I have extra that you can bring home."

"Brent doesn't eat this stuff during the season, but I can share with some of the staff here, too. Did you want something to drink?" I gesture to the mini fridge. "I have water and maybe some ice tea or something in there."

She hops up and has the fridge open before I can get to my feet. "Water would be great."

I finish off the rest of the cupcake and swallow before asking. "What else did you bring?"

"Well, since you impressed me with Raoul's, I thought I could return the favor." She pops open one of the containers. "Los Tacos."

"Oh yeah, their marinated steak is the best."

"I got a few different options." She hands me a container. "This one's the steak, and then I got chicken and a quesadilla, too." She continues unpacking her bag, setting up my desk with napkins and forks and little salsa containers.

"You didn't have to do all this." I pull my chair around to the side so I'm not sitting at the head, lording over her or something.

"I wanted to." She puts a warm hand on my shoulder and waits for me to meet her gaze. Her eyes are serious, but she smiles before removing her hand. "Let me do something for you."

That shuts me up.

Once we've organized the food, we dig in.

"This is a nice setup you have here." She glances around the room.

I shrug. "It's work."

"Work with a view. And a couch."

"It folds out into a bed. I wasn't kidding about being here until sunrise. Thankfully, there's also a private bathroom."

She grimaces. "Yikes. So what is it that you and your dad do? I mean, I know you do the restaurant supplies and you told me about your grandpa, but what is your role here?"

"Boring stuff. Trust me, you don't want to hear about it."

"I do, though." She takes a bite of her taco and then meets my eyes, her gaze steady.

"Okay. Don't say I didn't warn you." I give her the rundown of my daily duties, from reviewing marketing proposals and prospective new clients to hiring staff and signing off on purchases.

Surprisingly, she asks questions and pays attention and is legitimately interested.

"Is this always what you wanted to do?" she asks.

"Sure. I mean, after the accident there wasn't anything else I really could do. And before that, I knew it was coming. It's tradition to keep the business in the family."

"What about Brent?"

I shake my head. "That was never going to happen. As soon as Brent started Pop Warner at six, it was clear that was his calling. He hasn't gone more than a couple hours without a football in his hands since. And I'm the oldest, so . . ." I shrug. "It's what I've known I was going to do ever since I was a kid."

She frowns, a small crease forming between her brows. "But didn't you have other dreams? I mean, even if you can't snowboard professionally and wander around the globe saying things like 'Dude that was hella sick' in the X Games, wasn't there anything else you thought about doing?"

"Not really."

"Not even in preschool?"

"I wanted to be a garbage truck man when I was five."

She laughs. "You know, they get great benefits." She finishes the last of the quesadilla and puts the trash in the bag she brought. Then she pulls out another cupcake and unwraps it.

"Yeah. They get to drive around in a giant truck. I think it would be fun. I used to wait outside every Friday morning for them to drive by and our garbage man would always bring me little candies and treats."

She swallows a bite of cupcake, her eyes on mine. "I wish I had my camera."

"Why?"

"You looked different for a second. Like . . ." Her eyes search my face, considering her words before she speaks. "You normally look like you have the weight of the world on you, but just then, for a second, it was all gone. Your eyes were lighter. Maybe you should pursue this garbage man dream."

I laugh, even though her words are making me self-conscious. "I can't leave the company. Too many people count on me."

"You know the world won't end if you change careers. It happens all the time."

I finish my last bite of taco and wipe my mouth with one of the napkins. "Was it hard for you to leave modeling?"

"No. I get to have twice the desserts and none of the guilt." She lifts her cupcake. "If I were still a model, I wouldn't be having a cupcake before and after dinner. But in some ways it was hard, so yes and no. It's always scary to try something new. There's always a risk, always growing pains when you move outside your comfort zone. But I think you have to ask yourself which worst-case scenario you would regret more: staying where you are and being miserable but secure, or risking it and losing everything."

Her words give me pause. What would I do if I could do anything?

Right now, I would lick the speck of frosting on her lip. The urge is so great I lean in her direction but then stop when I realize what I'm doing.

"You have a little frosting." I point at my upper lip. "Right there."

"Oh." She laughs and then her pink tongue sneaks out and licks it off. "Did I get it?"

I blink and turn away to hide my very physical reaction to the motion. "Yeah you got it."

Since I can't look at her right now and I definitely can't stand up and move away, I focus on cleaning up the mess we've made, shoving napkins and trash into the bag.

"Um, I better get going," she says.

Can she sense my awkward attraction? She probably feels bad for me. "I could order you a car."

"No, it's fine, I can get an Uber. I'm already on it." She taps on her phone for a few seconds before glancing over at me. "Starlee told me I should go to the game this weekend. Apparently there's some rumors swirling that Brent and I are faking it. Are you going?"

"The Sunday night game? Yeah I'll be there. We could go together." It's a terrible idea. I do not need to be around her any more than absolutely necessary.

"That would be great." Her relieved smile lightens something in my chest. "I've never been to a game. I have no idea where to go or what to do." She bites her bottom lip. "What should I wear?"

"I'll have one of Brent's jerseys sent to your apartment."

She nods. "That would make sense."

"And then I can pick you up on the way. We sit in one of the boxes up by the announcers."

"That's what Starlee said. I'll be sure to be noticed there." She rolls her eyes.

"Does it bother you? All the pretending?"

"It does and it doesn't." She shrugs and one slim shoulder pops out of the loose material of her long-sleeved shirt. "I don't like being deceptive, but I know how this industry works and if I can save someone from the claws of that psycho Marissa, I feel like I have to, you know? And Brent is such a nice guy."

I have to drag my eyes away from the exposed peachy skin.

She's talking about Brent.

Focus, Marc.

"He is. He's the best."

Her phone dings. "That's my ride."

"Thanks for the cupcakes. Let me walk you down."

"You don't have to do that."

"I want to."

She gathers up her stuff and we walk to the elevator in silence. Down in the lobby, I walk her past security, where she gives me a small smile with a quick goodbye.

I turn to head back to the elevators and nod at Stan, the security guard.

"She's a good one."

"Yeah," I say. "She is."

Chapter Eleven

In wisdom gathered over time I have found
that every experience is a form of exploration.
   –Ansel Adams

Marc

I've been to hundreds of Brent's games, from Pop Warner to high school and college games all the way to the professional football league.

But I have never, in my life, spent more time getting ready for one.

"You're an idiot," I tell my reflection after the third time I've returned to the bathroom in a vain attempt to fix the one strand of my hair that eternally sticks up in the back. "I'm like a grown-up version of Alfalfa. And I'm talking to myself. I'm an insane, grown-up Alfalfa."

Insane because I have a crush on my brother's girlfriend. Excuse me, my brother's *fake* girlfriend.

The reflection in the mirror tilts his head.

My brother's fake girlfriend who is also a model. Well, ex-model, but the fact that she is hot enough to have ever been a model to begin with means I have absolutely no chance with her. I know this.

Doesn't stop me from pushing down the wayward hair one more time and reapplying another coat of deodorant. It's not like she's going to be distracted by my hair when my face is enough to distract anyone.

I scheduled a car from the company to drive us to the game. The driver is waiting downstairs by the time I'm done getting ready and when I slide in the back seat, I give him Gwen's address. There's nowhere to park on her street so I have him circle the block while I run up to get her.

Picking her up at her door, just like a real date.

She would never date you, a spiteful voice insists.

The building is older and a little shabby, smack in the middle of Morningside Heights, on Broadway near the bridge. The neighborhood isn't bad. It's a fairly decent part of town if by "decent" you mean there are fewer criminals per capita than Rikers. The building's narrow entrance is between a Mexican eatery and an Indian grocer. I walk through the scented haze of curry and cumin, bypassing the buzzer by following an old lady with bulging pockets who barely notices me and doesn't care at all that a strange man has entered through the door behind her.

The plaster is cracked, the floors haven't been washed in this century, and when I get to Gwen's apartment, I nearly have a heart attack when I see the one flimsy lock on her door. This is the only thing separating her from imminent death?

Or something slightly less dramatic.

"Hey." She opens the door with a bright smile, the glow of it distracting me from the fact that she's wearing Brent's jersey — the one I had sent over — on top of some tight-fitting, dark jeans.

"Hey."

"I need to grab my purse." She only has to walk a few paces away to grab the item from the couch.

And then the view of her walking away distracts me from what I wanted to tell her.

Focus, Marc.

I avert my attention to her door. I can't fix the building, but I can fix this.

"I'm so excited, I've never been to a real live football game before. But did you see that article in *Stylz* this morning? Ugh, Marissa is such a . . ." She stops. "What are you doing?"

The door is still open and I mess with the lock, clicking it from unlocked to locked, watching it and testing its strength. "You should really get some better locks for your door."

"My . . . what?" Her brow furrows and her eyes blink once, then twice. Her adorable confusion would make me grin if I weren't worried about her getting murdered.

"Your door couldn't keep out a stiff breeze. You don't even have a chain or anything."

She laughs. "You sound like my sister. I told her I would get a new lock installed but I haven't had time." The smile drops off quickly when she sees that I'm not joking. "I'll take care of it."

I nod, but the frown is persistent.

"Stop worrying." She rolls her eyes and tugs on my arm. "Come on."

~*~

The car drops us off outside the stadium and we have to walk through tailgaters to get to the entrance.

People stream everywhere in team colors and jerseys with painted faces. There's stumbling drunks, partying coeds, and the smell of burgers and beers lingering in the air.

"Hey pretty lady, you want some of my riblets?" someone calls at us almost immediately. Well, at Gwen.

I'm ready to put my head down and keep walking, but she surprises me by responding to the paunchy middle-aged guy in a Sharks jersey. "Only if my friend can have some, too."

He must nod or make some kind of sign of agreement, because she grabs my arm and tugs me in the direction of the tailgaters on our right.

"I don't know if this is a good idea."

"Come on," she says, pushing out her bottom lip and widening her eyes pleadingly.

I immediately relent. I'd probably chop off my right leg if she asked me to while making that pouty face.

Mr. Riblet eyes me as we approach. "Is this your boyfriend?" he asks.

We share a glance. "No, it's my boyfriend's brother."

"Oh girl, you playin' dirty!"

Some of his friends laugh and whoop behind him.

"His brother is Brent Crawford."

Mr. Riblet's eyes swing toward me, an overly exaggerated, comical movement.

"Marc Crawford." I hold out my hand, which he doesn't so much as glance at.

I've never seen anyone's eyes grow so wide so quickly. "Holy shit, that's right! I've seen you in interviews. I recognize you now. Your brother is the Superman? Benny! Benny, get over here! You want a toke on this, man?"

I politely decline the joint he tries to hand me, but it doesn't matter because all his buddies are coming over and shaking my hand, taking selfies with both of us, and shoving plates of food in our direction.

"My cousin will never believe this! Can I put this on Facebook?"

We spend another half hour with tailgaters. Most of them end up in a circle around Gwen, hanging on her every word and staring at her like she invented cold fusion. Or like she's a super-hot former model. I probably look exactly the same every time she's in my general vicinity. But it's more than her appearance. She's genuinely nice. She listens to everyone, focuses on whoever is speaking, and asks questions like she truly cares about the answer.

I'm in so much trouble.

Eventually, we leave our new friends and make our way into the stadium and up to the box.

After showing our IDs at the door, we get in. The box isn't huge, but it's split into two levels, which helps add to the space. On the top level, there's a small bar fully stocked with drinks and appetizers set out on a counter. Down a few steps are four rows of seats, with about a half a dozen chairs per row.

There are quite a few people already there, and most of them are hanging around the bar. I don't know any of them. I think they're mostly wives and relatives of the other players. We get a couple of glances and then they ignore us.

We skip the food—both still full from our tailgating experience—and find seats near the front of the box where we can watch right as the coin toss starts the game.

"This is great. I wish I would have come to a game sooner," she says.

"They are fun." But I don't mean it. I mean, I enjoy the games and I love supporting my brother, but it's even better with her. I never would have made friends with some random people roasting pig and smoking weed if I had come alone. I would have marched through the revelry to get to my destination, avoiding staring eyes.

"It makes living in New York fun again."

There's a pause in our conversation as Brent takes the field and we get up to cheer. And then there's a shot of us, the camera catching our movements through the glass of the box on the giant TV screen at the top of the field.

I wait until the camera pans back to the field and we're sitting down again to ask, "When did it stop being fun? Living in New York?"

"When I realized the truth about the people I thought were my friends."

"Was it because of Mr. Cheekbones?"

She smiles. "Lucky? He was part of it. The modeling world became . . ." She shakes her head. "I don't know, it was like I was living in this bubble where everything was about the way you look, the people you know, your weight, your height, not even things you can control. Everything I thought I knew became a lie." She speaks quietly; I almost can't hear her above the buzz of the crowd.

I want to press her for more, but now is not the time. And Brent is catching touchdowns.

As we watch Brent lead his team to a 32–27 victory, the conversation lightens and she tells me about her dream to travel the world, taking pictures.

"Like photojournalism?"

"Sort of. There's an indigenous culture in the middle of Pakistan that's endangered and I want to create a photo essay of their traditions. A human-interest piece capturing their day-to-day lives and customs. There are a ton of cultures slowly disappearing around the world. My dream is to travel and capture some of their moments before they're gone. I've been trying to get someone to take on the project, but I keep getting turned down. It's hard to be taken seriously when you don't look like a serious artist."

"I would read that story. Even though you are terribly good-looking, I wouldn't let that stand in my way."

She chuckles. "I wish more editors agreed with you. I also wish Marissa would stop with her articles. Starlee hooked me up with a magazine interview over the phone this morning, and instead of asking about my idea, they asked about my relationship with Brent."

"Oh, no."

"Oh, yes. I kept trying to change the subject to the project I've been working on locally—it's a piece on endangered languages—but they just kept going back to Brent and how I felt about the investigation and could I get him to come talk to them. It was a nightmare."

"I'm sorry you're having to deal with that. And now I want to know about endangered languages. What does that mean, exactly?"

Her face brightens. "It's really fascinating, actually. In countries around the globe, languages are dying off as people assimilate and move, but immigrants who came to New York generations ago are still passing some of these languages down."

"That's insane."

"It really is. There's an organization here, the Endangered Language Alliance, and I've been taking shots of the linguists and people who still speak the languages that they're working to preserve. My hope is to connect this project to the endangered cultures when I go abroad . . . if I ever get the chance."

Our conversation is cut off as Brent catches another touchdown pass and our box explodes in a frenzy of clapping and shouting.

There's no more time for conversation. The box has gotten more and more packed as the night's gone on. Now the noise is riotous and the game is nearly over.

Once it ends, we escape the box to meet Brent downstairs. It takes a little bit of time getting through the crowds, but we would have to wait anyway for Brent to get changed.

When we get down to the locker room door, we have to wait even longer. There's press coming in and out. Some of them stop and snap pictures of Gwen.

She puts on a good show, smiling for the pics, but I can see the tension in her jaw.

Finally, Brent exits into the hallway. Gwen runs up and hugs him, continuing the charade.

But then he bends down slightly and kisses her on the mouth. And it goes on for a bit.

Gwen stiffens, then relaxes into the embrace and my heart tugs in my chest.

Does she want to kiss him?

Is she enjoying this?

Maybe I imagined that initial tensing of muscles and resistance.

After what feels like hours but is probably only a handful of seconds, they break apart.

Cameras are flashing and snapping. Some of the reporters are tossing out questions about their relationship and demands for more public displays.

They both play it off, yelling no comment with a laugh, linking hands, and heading away from the gaggle of press toward the parking garage.

And like the thirdest wheel on the most awkward of vehicles, I follow them.

Brent's car is parked at the stadium, a black Porsche Panamera.

It's a sleek and sexy car and he looks great in it.

I get in the back seat.

We head to Gwen's apartment, and they laugh together the entire drive. Gwen tells Brent about our tailgating experience and he talks about some of the things that happened on the sidelines during the game.

There's an open parking spot down the block near Gwen's building. I stay in the car and Brent goes with her to her front door.

I can't see them from here.

It's no big deal.

It's not like they're going to make out or something while I'm waiting. After all, that shot in front of the cameras was just that, for the cameras. Right?

But still. I move into the front seat and then wait in quiet agony until Brent reappears moments later.

"Dude, her apartment has like no security," he says.

"I know, that's what I told her."

"We need to take care of that."

"I was planning on it first thing tomorrow morning."

He nods, comfortable in the knowledge that I'm on top of it. "I invited her to Connecticut next week for the holiday."

"You did?"

"Yeah. *Stylz* published an article this morning that our relationship is all a ruse."

"What is it with that magazine?"

"Marissa. I got word today that she's not cooperating with the Sharks' investigation. Something Starlee is having a field day with. She's getting counter articles written to point out that little factoid, but she wants more."

"Marissa must be obsessed with you."

He shrugs. "I guess. Anyway, we have to step it up and make it seem more legit. It's my fault. The season is always crazy. And we hardly ever show public displays of affection. Plus we've only gone out places we know we will be seen where the paparazzi are likely to lurk."

"Is that why you . . . ?"

He grimaces slightly. "Yeah. Was it obvious? I apologized just now and explained to her why I kissed her like that without warning. She understood. She's so cool and laid back, you know? We text sometimes when I'm on the road and she's so sweet."

I have to swallow before I answer. "That's cool."

What have they been texting about? Business stuff? The messages we've been sending back and forth are pretty innocent. Are theirs? What if they're sexting? I shove the thought aside. It's really none of my business. Then why do I suddenly want to punch my brother in the mouth?

"I don't think I would mind if this fake relationship took a turn into reality," Brent says, and my stomach heaves. I don't think it's from the barbeque.

It shouldn't bother me or surprise me. They would be perfect together. They're two of the most beautiful people I've ever seen in real life. They make sense.

Gwen and I? Not so much.

"Thanks for spending time with her while I've been on the road and busy with games. It means a lot to me," he adds.

I nod and mumble something that sounds like you're welcome.

If only he knew.

Chapter Twelve

A good snapshot keeps a moment from running away.
      –Eudora Welty

Gwen

Brent and Marc pick me up at eight o'clock sharp on Thanksgiving morning. The day before, Marc came over with dinner for my neighbor Martha and a new lock for my door.

We had been exchanging emails again. I'd happened to mention how I felt bad leaving Martha on her own over the holidays. I didn't ask him to do anything, but he brought over some precooked, fancy Thanksgiving feast for one from a restaurant they work with. It even has heating instructions on it. Then he stood in my doorway and installed a new lock himself.

"You didn't have to do all of this," I told him.

"I wanted to."

The thing is, he really did. I had been working late all week, taking jobs that foot the bills and also spending time at the Endangered Language Alliance for my project. But he had other obligations, too. And still, he manages to take care of everyone, Brent, his dad, his business, a bunch of kids that aren't even his, and now me.

And I'm going to be in a car with him for over two hours.

Him and his brother.

His brother that I'm dating.

Fake dating.

Brent meets me at the front door of my building and I follow him to where the car is parked. Marc is there, opening the trunk of the Porsche. I bring my bag over and set it in the back.

"This is all you have?" he asks.

"We're staying for one night, right?" I shade my eyes from the morning sun and squint at him. I only packed one extra outfit for tomorrow, yoga pants to sleep in, and my toiletry items.

"Yeah. There's Brent's bag." He gestures to a giant suitcase next to my little bag. Beside it is a small backpack that must be Marc's.

I laugh. Brent's suitcase is at least three times the size of my little sack.

"Hey, I have to fly out early tomorrow for practice," Brent protests.

"I'm just messing with you, bro." Marc shuts the trunk. "You want shotgun?" he asks me.

"I'll take the back seat. That way I can sleep."

"Smart lady."

Brent gets behind the wheel and Marc gets in the passenger side. Then we're off.

We haven't even made it out of the city before they start bickering over the music. Brent wants to listen to reggae and Marc wants to listen to classic rock.

But eventually Brent gets his way—not shocking—and while the Hudson disappears from view, Bob Marley starts singing about three little birds pitched by his doorstep.

The first leg of the trip goes by quickly while I ask them about our destination and what to expect. We've already discussed that Brent and I have to keep up the charade in front of the Hamiltons. No one can know it's all a ruse.

"You guys grew up in Kent?" I ask.

"Yeah," Brent answers. "There's a few boarding schools nearby that Dad wanted to send us to, but Mom didn't want to be far away so they bought a house there. That way we could go to the fancy school but still live at home."

There's a world of unspoken truths in that statement—that perfectly describes their relationship with their dad vs. their relationship with their mom. Something I had already gotten a sense of from all of their previous comments, or lack thereof in Marc's case. And that was *before* I met their dad.

"The Hamiltons were your mom's best friends?"

"Jenny and Dan lived next door to them growing up," Marc says. "They have three kids. The guys are close to our age, but Janice was a surprise—she's still in high school. They're pretty awesome. One of their sons, Luke, should be there with his wife, Becky, and their son, but Ian is finishing up medical school in California."

"How old is Luke's son?"

"Becky just had a baby boy, Colin, a few months ago."

They ask about what my family does for the holidays and I explain that my parents have never really been into Thanksgiving, but that all changed when my sister hooked up with Sam. Sam's family really gets crazy for Thanksgiving, and every other opportunity to get together and eat a bunch of food. I think they even celebrate Flag Day.

"Seriously, they have like thirty people to their house for dinner. I don't know how Sam's mom does it. He has two brothers and a sister, and they all have spouses, then there's grandparents and cousins and kids running around like hooligans. It's crazy."

"Sounds like fun," Marc says. "I've always wanted to have a big family. Instead we have to ingratiate ourselves with our neighbor's clan."

Brent nods. "And we can't even get Dad to recognize our birthdays, let alone hang out with us over the holidays."

Marc glances over at him sharply, surprised. At the comment, or at the fact that Brent said it out loud?

"Has he always been like that?" I ask.

"When Mom was alive," Marc angles his head toward me so I can hear him better, pointing the unscarred side of his face in my direction, "Dad was around more. I don't think he necessarily wanted to go to family functions, but she would force him into things. And I think once he was there he had a pretty good time. Ever since she died, he kind of gave up."

"That's sad."

Brent gives a small laugh. "I don't think he's sad spending time on the beach with his latest swimsuit model."

Marc nods. "Yeah, I don't know. He acts like he's happy, but he doesn't seem happy. Do you know what I mean?"

"Um. No." Brent clicks on the blinker and checks his blind spot before merging into the next lane.

"I'm kind of worried I'm going to end up like him," Marc says, the words quiet.

Brent laughs. "You will never be like that guy."

"I don't know. I mean, maybe he never wanted to work at Crawford and Company. He was forced into it by his dad and he felt like he couldn't leave, and that's why he clings to it so much now. He gave up everything for it."

"Is that what you feel like? Like you've given something up?" Brent asks.

Marc shrugs. "I don't know anymore. When I see the future spread out before me and it involves a corner office with a ton of paperwork . . . I don't know if I want that to be my life."

"Maybe not the rest of your life, but someone has to take care of Dad. And who would run the company when he's gone?"

It's clear to me in that moment that although Brent doesn't mean anything by the words—and he's not wrong, it is a family business, and he really is concerned for his dad—he also doesn't realize the implications of what he's asking of Marc.

"You're right," Marc says quietly before turning his gaze out the passenger window.

Marc is a rock, Brent told me.

Marc is the rock because there is no one else. He steps up and does what he has to do for his family. And for everyone else around him. With little to no regard for himself.

My chest squeezes for him, for this scarred man who hides so much of himself.

I speak up from the back seat. "I think you should do whatever will make you happy. Screw the company. Screw your dad. You can find someone else to manage it. Why not just have ownership interest and sell half of it or something? Don't corporations do that all the time?"

"It's not that easy," Brent says.

I frown. Brent's so used to Marc handling everything and acting as a buffer for their dad. What about what Marc wants?

Marc changes the subject, turning the conversation over to football and Brent's teammates. They chat about people I don't know and eventually I doze off, listening to the drone of the tires on the pavement and the soothing sound of deep voices.

~*~

"We're here."

I blink my eyes open and find both brothers turned in their seats watching me.

"Oh, sorry." I wipe my eyes and try to tamp down the embarrassment at being so vulnerable in front of two hot guys.

"You're cute when you sleep." Brent's crooked smile is all sweetness and charm.

"You drool." Marc's deadpan makes me chuckle.

Brent hits him in the shoulder but Marc winks at me and then they both slide out of the car.

I stretch for a minute before unfolding myself out of the back seat.

We're at the top of the driveway, parked near a detached garage. The Hamiltons' house is a large two story with a white picket fence and a deep front porch. A bunch of trees surround the expansive property. They probably look amazing when they're full of leaves, but they're bare bones right now.

Marc grabs my bag, but Brent takes it from him and carries it up the steps. Which makes me think . . . "About those sleeping arrangements?"

"We'll have separate rooms," Brent assures me.

I nod in relief, glad we aren't expected to keep up the charade that far. Why didn't I think of this before?

"Unless," he adds with a brow wag, "you get lonely and need company."

Marc hits him in the shoulder.

I follow them up to the front door and Brent knocks. "No need to get punchy," he says to Marc while rubbing his arm.

"I promise to restrain myself unless you totally deserve it. Which you did for that douchebag comment."

I smile, secretly pleased that Marc is so concerned with my honor.

The door swings open.

"Brent!" A dark-haired teen girl in a flimsy tank top and yoga pants flings herself into Brent's arms.

"Janice, how are you?" Brent hugs her, awkwardly patting her back and not so subtly trying to extricate himself from her embrace.

Marc steps past them into the entryway and I follow his lead. "Nice to see you, too," Marc says drily but Janice doesn't notice.

I can't help but giggle and then take a moment to glance around. From the vaulted entryway, it's clear the house is tastefully decorated. There are cream-colored walls and white wainscoting, thick rugs that cover the hardwood floors, and pictures of kids peppering the walls. The whole setup emanates security and home.

"Who's this?"

Brent has managed to disconnect himself from Janice and she's eyeing me with more than a little hostility. "I'm Gwen, Brent's girlfriend." I stick out a hand.

"Nice to meet you." Her handshake is limp. "Hi, Marc." She finally acknowledges him with a wave. No hug.

"Where is everyone?" Brent asks her.

She aims her bright smile at Brent. "They're in the game room setting up for the championship."

"Championship?" I ask.

"Every year we have an Uno contest," Marc explains.

"There's a whole setup with a chalkboard and a tournament bracket and everything."

"Sounds like fun."

"Boys! You made it." A woman comes into the entryway from the back of the house. She's petite with dark hair like Janice, except her beaming smile is aimed at all of us and not just at Brent. She hugs Marc first, then Brent, and then she hugs me, too. "You must be Gwen, I've heard so much about you."

"You have?" Marc asks.

"Well, I've heard a little about you from Brent and the rest I've read online."

I grimace. "That's a little scary."

"Oh, I only believe the good stuff," she assures me. "Let's not keep you guys by the door all day. I'll show you where your rooms are so you can put your bags down and get freshened up. There's brunch—omelets and waffles and fruit—it's all in the kitchen if you guys are hungry."

"That sounds amazing."

We follow her up the wide staircase that leads from the entry to the upper floor and she talks the entire time. "I'm putting you guys in the boys' old rooms so you'll be sharing the connecting bathroom, and Gwen, you get the guest room." She keeps going, talking about how they're smoking a turkey for dinner and how big Luke's babies are getting.

We stop in front of my room first and I escape inside with a quick thanks, shutting the door behind me. I toss my bag and then myself on the soft-looking comforter of the queen-sized bed.

This is going to be interesting.

~*~

I spend about twenty minutes gathering my wits and getting comfortable in the guest room before I head downstairs.

I find Jenny in the kitchen, where she introduces me to her daughter-in-law, her son Luke's wife, Becky. They look like they've stepped out of a Lands' End catalogue in coordinating sweater sets and mom bobs, but Becky's smile is genuine and she greets me with a hug, just like Jenny did.

"It's so nice to meet you. Are you hungry? We ate brunch already but we saved some for you and the guys."

"I'm starved actually. I skipped breakfast."

Jenny shows me a side table where they've set up a little belgian waffle station with different toppings, along with fruit and an assortment of pastries.

"This looks amazing. Thank you for going to all this trouble."

Jenny waves a hand at me. "It's nothing. Here, let me show you how the waffle maker works."

She helps me create a stack of waffles covered in chocolate sauce and strawberries and whipped cream.

Marc and Brent come downstairs and pile up plates of their own, so I don't feel too self-conscious stuffing my face in front of Becky and Jenny.

I listen and eat while they all catch up on happenings around the neighborhood and within their respective families. Jenny asks me questions occasionally about my own family and what they're doing for the holidays so I don't feel like the odd man out.

Once we've finished eating, Luke comes into the kitchen. He's a handsome guy, with dark hair and square-shaped glasses. He has a sleeping baby strapped to his chest, a chunky little guy wearing a onesie covered in cartoon turkeys. Luke kisses his wife on the cheek before coming over to shake my hand.

Jenny gives me a tour of the house — which Brent and Marc decide to crash. After she shows me around the house, I meet Dan in the backyard where he's watching the smoker, which basically involves him sitting on a lounge chair bundled up in a coat and beanie with a beer in his hand. He greets me with as much warmth as the rest of the family, though. And that's the part of the tour where we lose the guys.

"Does it really need to be watched?" I ask Jenny when we're back in the kitchen, just her, Becky, and I.

"No. It's what he likes to pretend to do, when really he's out there sneaking cigars with the guys."

"Kind of like what we're doing in here," Becky laughs. "Minus the cigars."

There's not much work to be done in the kitchen. Jenny already made pie and prepped all of the side dishes for dinner.

"And now," she says, "we hang out in the kitchen pretending there's so much to do when really we just talk and drink mimosas."

"I can get behind that."

Luke comes in then and hands the baby off to Becky before disappearing back outside.

"We take turns," she tells me.

"Your son is so beautiful." I watch him yawn in her arms, his little mouth stretching and his tiny fingers reaching.

"Do you want to hold him?"

"Can I? Let me wash my hands first. I haven't held someone so tiny since my niece and nephews were little." I put my mimosa down and wash up before holding out my arms to take him.

She gently hands him over and I make sure to take care with his head, adjusting until he's safely in the crook of my arm, watching me with big eyes and attempting to grab at my hair.

"Watch out, he's strong. He'll pull those beautiful blonde locks right out."

"It's fine, I'm used to it."

"I bet you're a great aunt," Jenny says, her smile widening. She winks at Becky.

Becky laughs. "What she's trying to say is you'll be a great mom when you and Brent get married and have super-hot babies."

Heat fills my face. "We're not getting married. We've barely started dating."

"Yeah, but he hasn't brought anyone home since Bella," Jenny says. "And don't tell anyone, but I never liked that girl. Too insecure. Too much of a pushover. I bet one of her friends convinced her to break up with Brent and she followed like a lemming. You're much more assertive, I can tell."

"You were best friends with their mom, right?" I've been itching to get more information on Marc's mom and his childhood.

She nods. "I know I'm like a second mom to those boys, but Cindy's shoes are hard to fill."

"Brent and Marc have talked about her. It sounds like she was an amazing woman."

"She was," Jenny agrees. "She did more for those kids than anyone could imagine. She worked to keep them down-to-earth. Even though they had money to live in the biggest of mansions, they grew up here. Just next door. It was important to her that they had a normal childhood, not like their dad."

"Mr. Crawford didn't have a normal childhood?" I ask.

"He grew up in the city. Cindy always felt like having all that money thrown at him his whole life made him a bit broken somehow. His parents cared more about appearances than anything else. And they fought like crazy, both passionate and hot-tempered. They never got along with each other. I think it gave Albert a distorted view of what a real relationship should be like."

"That's kind of sad," Becky says.

"They loved each other a lot, but Albert's dad sort of poisoned him against her."

"How so?" I ask.

She shrugs. "It seemed to me that he was jealous, since his own life had been all about the business and not about his family. He resented that Albert tried to have the best of both worlds. Anyway, Cindy always made sure Marc and Brent weren't just thrown to tutors and given everything they wanted. And she showered them with affection and love. Any material things, she made them work for. Her own family was poor, which was another point of contention between Albert and his father."

"I get the impression Albert has gotten even more distant since Cindy died," I say.

Jenny nods. "He really loved her, but who wouldn't? She was like Snow White. She was the glue that held him to what was important when the business tried to take over his life."

The back door opens and a few seconds later Marc pops into the kitchen. "Can I help you ladies with anything?"

"You know boys aren't allowed in here," Becky says.

He sees me holding the baby and walks over to us, putting his finger in Colin's palm so his little hand flexes and closes around it. "There's already a boy in here."

"Babies don't count. They can't repeat our conversations."

"You don't want us in here so you can talk about us."

"Finally, he gets it."

Marc leans into my shoulder, rubbing a thumb against Colin's head. "He's so sweet."

"He is." I watch Marc's eyes warm and crinkle and my heart melts a little bit more in my chest.

He meets my eyes and for a couple of seconds everything else disappears.

Then Colin farts against my arm.

We freeze for a second and then burst into laughter.

"Sorry," Becky says. "He's a little tooting machine after he eats."

I wave off her apology, still sharing the moment with Marc.

His eyes linger on my face before he steps away. "Well, and with that gassy accompaniment, I am out of here. I can tell when I'm not wanted."

"We love you, Marc," Jenny calls to his back as he leaves the kitchen. "So," she turns to me. "Who is Marc dating now that Marissa is out of the picture?"

"No one. I don't think."

"Poor guy, he spends all his time working."

"Just like his dad," Becky mutters.

Janice emerges from her room, where she'd been hiding, and Jenny changes the subject. We chat about other things until the turkey is ready.

Dinner is excellent. We eat in the formal dining room, but it's not stuffy, and conversation is comfortable. It's easy to see why Brent and Marc spend their holidays here.

Afterward, everyone files into the den for the Uno championship.

I lose in the first round and then sit back and watch for a while.

When Luke goes to put the baby to sleep—he's already been passed out in his chest carrier for a couple hours—I decide to make my own escape.

"I need to call my family," I use as my excuse. It's only six back home, so everyone should be around.

"I'll walk you up," Brent says. "I have an early flight and a long day of practice tomorrow."

Everyone gets up and there's a bunch of hugging and kissing and goodnight wishes before we're allowed to leave the room.

"No hanky-panky in the halls," Becky calls.

"They're not going to do that." Janice rolls her eyes.

Once we're at my door, I have my hand on the knob to escape but Brent stops me with a hand on my arm. I turn and face him.

"I'm glad you came with us. I hope you're having a good time."

"They're an awesome family. Thanks for inviting me."

There's a tense moment. His hand is still on my arm and then it happens.

He leans.

There's no one watching. What is he doing?

I tense. Is he going to kiss me?

But then his head moves up and his lips press softly against my forehead. After a quick second, he pulls back.

"Sleep good," he says. His eyes are searching mine, but I don't think he's going to find what he wants to see.

Once safely ensconced in the guest room, I resist the urge to bang my head against the wall.

What the fuck was that? Is Brent . . . ?

No. Not possible. It's just the holidays and maybe he's a little lonely.

That's got to be it. After all, he can't be interested in . . . well, you know.

I pick up my cell phone and call Gemma. As soon as she answers, voices and laughter filter through the earpiece from the background.

"Happy Thanksgiving!" she calls into the phone.

"Who's that?" someone asks.

"It's Gwen."

"Happy Thanksgiving!" comes the chorus.

"Are you having fun? Tell me what's going on," she says.

I give her an update and assure her that I'm being treated well, I've consumed at least twice my body weight in turkey, and I have a room to myself. I want to talk to her about the awkward moment with Brent in the hall, but I can't. I can't talk to anyone about it. I can't even fudge the story. After all, they might think it's weird that I don't want to kiss the guy I'm supposed to be dating.

She passes me around to Gabby, who then passes me to Mom, who then passes me back to Gemma.

"I love you, have fun, call me when you get home."

We hang up and in the ensuing silence, I find myself staring at my reflection in the mirror above the dresser.

I can't stop thinking about the moment in the hall with Brent. Dear God, please don't let him have feelings for me.

I get ready for bed and try to read on my phone to settle my thoughts but I can't focus on the words.

I'm too pent up. There's only one thing I can think of to save me.

I need pie.

Chapter Thirteen

The thing that's important to know is that you never know. You're always sort of feeling your way.

    –Diane Arbus

Marc

I've always been comfortable with the Hamiltons. They're the only family I've ever known.

But right now, there's a monkey under my skin itching to break out.

Brent walked Gwen up to her room fifteen minutes ago.

I'm sure they both went to their respective beds. Mostly sure.

Or maybe he's in her room right now, removing her clothes, kissing her neck, a malevolent voice whispers.

Images flash in my mind like evil gremlins, and I shove them away. Because of the distraction, I lose the last game of Uno to Becky. And then one by one, people head to bed. By the time I make it to my room, the house is quiet.

Brent's room and mine are attached by a bathroom. When I go in to brush my teeth and get ready for bed, I stick my head against his door. Right away the soft vibration of Brent snoring reaches me, the sound releasing a bit of tension I've been holding since he and Gwen went to bed.

Of course nothing is really happening, but I remember what he said the other night. He wouldn't mind if there was something there. Maybe he just has an inkling. It doesn't mean he has *real* feelings for her, right? Would he have told me if he did?

It's not like I've mentioned my own thoughts, but that's only because it's never going to happen and I've been embarrassed and shamed enough when it comes to women. After all, even Brent doesn't believe anything could happen with me and Gwen.

My thoughts are turning me into a loser.

Time to eat my feelings.

Downstairs, the oven light is on, casting a soft glow over the kitchen and highlighting a figure standing next to the counter with a fork in her hand. She doesn't see me at first, too busy digging into the pie tin in front of her, taking small bites and then doing a cute little shimmy each time.

I lean in the doorway and watch for a couple of seconds before laughter overtakes me.

She startles and turns at the sound.

"Get your hands off my pie," I say.

She lifts it up and looks at it from different angles, as if searching for something. "Excuse me, but I don't see your name on it. Did you come down here to commandeer the desserts?"

"I did, but I see you've beat me to it."

"Here." She opens a drawer and pulls out a fork, holding it in my direction. "We can share."

Walking toward her, I know, somewhere in my bones, this is going to be about more than sharing food in a dark kitchen in the middle of the night. The thought doesn't stop me from walking over and taking the proffered fork.

"You can have this side, and I get this side." She motions down the center of the pie with a finger.

Over the next few minutes we stand together, digging into opposite sides of the pie with nothing but than the occasional clink of our forks against the pan disrupting the comfortable silence.

But then her utensil starts creeping closer and closer to my side. I watch it with interest, and when she finally passes the invisible center divider, I halt her progress with my own fork. "En guard."

A laugh bubbles up in her throat and she reclaims her utensil, holding it up like a sword.

We clash a couple times before we're both laughing and nudging each other to keep it quiet.

"You're really good at fork fencing," she says after our laughter has subsided and we're back to eating the pie.

"Maybe that will be my new career. Think it has potential?"

"I think you could corner the market on using forks as a deadly weapon. Are you really thinking about it? Leaving your dad's company?"

"I don't know. Maybe Brent's right and it's a bad idea. I want to do it, but . . . who would take care of everything at the company?"

"What if you pick your replacement? Then you can make sure they're good enough."

"But they'd also have to be able to take on my dad. Not many are up for that level of babysitting."

"You'll never know unless you try."

"Maybe you're right."

We're standing really close. So close I can see the rise and fall of her chest as she breathes out and catch a whiff of her shampoo—vanilla and honey—when I breathe in.

"It's not just about the company. Don't think of me as less than a man for admitting this, but it's scary to step out of my comfort zone and into the unknown."

Her eyes don't leave mine when she speaks. "You are one of the best men I've ever met. You could never be less than anyone."

I don't know how to respond to that. Thankfully, I don't have to because she keeps talking.

"I didn't know if I would make it as a photographer, but leaving the modeling world was the best decision I've ever made. Besides midnight pie." She holds up a pie-filled fork. "Most things worth having are worth fighting for."

"Are they?"

Our eyes meet and I wait for her to look away, but she doesn't.

I put my fork on the counter. She puts hers down, too, her eyes never leaving mine.

I'm not sure who reaches first. There's mutual grabbing and then she's in my arms.

The same place I've been imagining her for weeks.

Her lips are softer than I imagined. Her hands are on my shoulders, gently pulling me closer. My fingers are on her waist, feeling the warmth of her skin under her thin shirt.

Our lips pull together softly, gently, everything in slow motion, and then her tongue slips into my mouth.

She's sweet and tart, better than the half-eaten pie on the counter. Like honey and sunshine.

Her hands cup my face, trying to get closer still.

My limbs have developed a mind of their own. I can't stop from reaching down and grabbing her ass and pulling her into me. More. She needs to be so much closer.

Without shoes she's only a couple inches shorter than me and I'm slayed by how perfectly her body curves into mine.

She pulls back on a gasp. "Marc." The word is full of want and regret.

It's the regret that stops me short. "I'm sorry."

I don't know why I'm apologizing. I'm the least sorry I've ever been, but it seems like the right thing to say now, like maybe what she wants to hear? It's also the biggest lie I've ever uttered.

She pulls away even farther, until my hands drop to my sides, bereft.

"It's okay." Without another word, she slips backward, not meeting my eyes, crossing her arms over her chest.

After a pause, she turns and flees the room.

Although the oven light is still shining, the cozy warmth is gone.

In a daze, I put the pie back in the fridge and the forks in the sink. I'm not hungry anymore.

What kills me is the regret in her eyes. What does she regret, exactly? That it was me? Or something more palatable, like maybe because of what she told me about her career goals and leaving the city and not wanting anything serious.

I was a fool to kiss her. And keep kissing her. And touching her. And wanting her. But I did. I do. It's not just the fact that she's gorgeous. She's kind and smart and funny and everything about her is beautiful. My fingers feel the loss of her skin like a missing limb.

What have I done?

Chapter Fourteen

Don't think too much. The best pictures come naturally.
   –Chiara Ferragni

Gwen

The next day, Brent's gone when I wake up. Marc and I will be driving back to the city. Alone together for almost two hours.

What was I thinking?

I was thinking that Marc is the most attractive person I've ever known, and I want to sit in his lap, kiss him senseless, and then do other, dirtier things that I can't think about without bursting into flames right here and now. Why is this happening? I don't want or need complications.

I'm supposed to be focusing on my career.

And for crying out loud, I'm supposed to be dating his brother. I have to forget that thing I can't stop thinking about ever happened. But how can I do that when the phantom taste of his lips on mine is so strong, so sweet and soft and sincere?

I stuff a sweater into my bag and yank the zipper shut. It's not like we could happen even if I wasn't planning on leaving the country. Can you imagine? First I date Brent, then suddenly I'm showing up with his brother? Everyone would know it's a scam. That would ruin Brent. I like Brent. But not like I like Marc. And none of this is relevant anyway because I'm leaving New York as soon as I can.

Then why are you still thinking about it?

"Uuugh, I am so fucked."

"Did you say something?" Janice is standing outside my door, watching me, her eyes guarded and suspicious.

"I said I like trucks."

"That doesn't sound like what you said." She leans against my doorframe, full of teen arrogance and jealousy. "So you're driving home with Marc today?"

"Yep."

"You know, he's a really great guy."

"Yeah, I know."

"Maybe even better than Brent, in a lot of ways."

I know she's trying to turn me from Brent. Young crushes are so heartbreaking. But it's still an echo of my own thoughts.

"Are you almost ready?" Marc is suddenly next to Janice in the doorway and when I meet his eyes, my stomach drops. He's freshly showered, making his hair darker than normal, but he didn't shave so there's the perfect bit of stubble around his mouth and along his jaw. I've never seen it. before He's always so clean-shaven. The added bit of scruff makes him look even sexier than usual. I wonder what it would feel like against my face. Or my chest. Or lower.

I swallow. He asked me a question.

"Yes."

He nods, smiles softly, and then turns and walks down the hall.

After Janice rolls her eyes at me, she turns and follows him.

I take a deep breath.

I can do this.

Jenny packs us a small cooler full of leftovers. The entire family comes outside to say goodbye and there are hugs and kisses and then we get in the car.

We're silent as he maneuvers the car through the neighborhood and I watch the houses pass by.

It's the most uncomfortable silence I've ever had with Marc, and it's my own fault. I need to stop thinking about last night.

I wonder if he feels the same because he tinkers with the radio for what seems like forever before finally settling on some classic rock.

"No reggae this time?"

"Did you want to listen to something else?"

"No. This is fine."

More silence.

Should I mention the kiss? He isn't mentioning it. He said he was sorry. He obviously regrets it. Maybe he's like most of the men I've met: he's attracted to me, but there's nothing beyond looks or what they could get from me to use for their own benefit. Maybe that's really all I have to offer. Or maybe it's like Lucky, a way to control and manipulate. But no, Marc isn't like that. Right?

I want to ask him. The question is on the tip of my tongue — *Are you really sorry about last night?* But I can't do it. I can't put myself out there like that. What if he says no? Or what if he says yes?

That might be worse. The feelings growing inside me are new and fragile, like the most delicate flower in the middle of a thunderstorm. Can I trust myself? I thought what Lucky and I had was real, too. In fact, I thought I was in love with that motherfucker. I'm not exactly the best judge of character.

"What are you doing for the rest of the weekend?"

I shrug. "Working. You?"

"Same."

Silence.

He clears his throat. "There's a Citgo up here that Brent and I stop at for the most unhealthy road snacks we can find. Want something?"

"Sure."

The Citgo is a typical gas station convenience store, rows of sodium-infused snacks, candy, a soda machine in the corner, and a row of glass refrigerators in the back.

We head down one of the aisles. Marc reaches out and grabs a box of Zingers and tosses them to me.

"Pumpkin-flavored Zingers?" I grimace. "I'm basic, but I'm not that basic."

He takes the box back. "They actually sound kind of good."

I laugh. "You eat them then."

"I will. And I bet you'll want one."

"I bet I won't."

We grab a few more things and get back in the car, and this time the silence is not quite so deafening.

"I'm glad you came with us," Marc says. "It's nice to have company on long drives. If you hadn't come with us, I'd be driving back alone."

"Well you can thank Marissa. If it wasn't for her articles, I wouldn't be here."

He chuffs. "I'm not sure we can give her credit for anything positive in our lives, but that's a good one."

I clear my throat. "Have you seen her at all since . . . ?"

"No. Thank God. We haven't heard so much as a peep from that corner, other than the article about you and Brent being a hoax." He glances over at me and then turns back to the road. "I'm sorry you've gotten dragged through the muck because of all this."

It's interesting to me that Marc is apologizing even though I'm doing this whole thing for Brent, right? "It isn't the first time Marissa has written bad things about me. I'll survive."

"You know, she talked to me about you. After we first met at the photo shoot."

"I can't say I'm surprised."

"She was worried about Brent dating you. Now I know the real reason why: she wanted him for herself."

"Did she say why she was worried?" I ask, against my better judgment.

"Something about how you were flighty and unreliable. I think those were her exact words."

I shake my head. "She's one to talk."

"My thoughts exactly. How did you meet her, anyway?"

"Oh, you know, when I was modeling, she was always around. And I think she's still friends with my ex, Lucky."

"Mr. Cheekbones? The guy we saw at Raoul's?"

"Yeah."

"Can I ask what happened with him?"

I shrug. "Not much to tell. He turned into a raging control freak who treated me like I was worth less than the scum on his shoe."

"How did you get involved with him to begin with?"

"I met him on a job when I first started getting work in the city. He was so . . . well-connected and confident and put together. I had never met anyone like him."

"And those cheekbones."

I smile at his sarcastic tone. Is he jealous? "He does have nice cheekbones. They're implants."

"Gross," he grumbles.

I sigh and continue. Might as well tell the whole story. "He was nice, at first. Modeling is a rough gig. There's a lot of expectations. Lucky understood all of that. He made my life easier. But then he changed. And the change happened slowly enough that I didn't notice it at first. It started with an offhand comment when I wanted to go out for a burger one night. Then it got worse and worse."

"He didn't want you to have a burger?"

"He didn't say it like that, it was more like . . . 'oh you know if you eat that you'll probably have to throw it up since you have a bikini shoot tomorrow.' "

"Are you kidding me?" His voice tightens, and the look he tosses me is filled with shock.

My chest twinges with shame. "It's hard to explain, but what he said wasn't *wrong*. It's what most models do. And after a while with a bunch of those comments adding up over time, mixed with him telling me how much I meant to him and how beautiful I was . . . it was like I was brainwashed. I had already been living in this world where looks are everything and Lucky used that to manipulate me."

"It was wrong for him to treat you that way."

"You're right. And that's why I left."

"I'm sorry." He reaches a hand in my direction, lightly squeezing my wrist, his eyes still on the road. "I don't mean to sound like you did anything wrong in any way. You didn't. He's the asshole. You're a strong person for getting out. A lot of people can't. How did you manage to leave?"

He leaves his hand on my wrist, warm and comforting, and it soothes some of the tightness in my chest.

"It started when I got the job with Victoria, which happened almost by accident. I had been taking a bunch of shots for fun, mostly of Lucky and some of our friends. I showed them to her and she loved them. Until then, I don't think Lucky really thought I would leave the industry. When I got the shoot with her, suddenly it was like everything was real. And then his behavior deteriorated. He was angry all the time about every little thing I did. It got to the point where he would get mad at me for going to lunch with a friend, or forgetting to put the cap on the toothpaste. He would convince me that I had done something terribly wrong, even though logically I knew that I hadn't."

I shut my eyes, remembering. Once the words start, I can't stop them. It's like the floodgates have opened and there's no way to shut them against the tide of water spilling out.

"I wanted to leave. I was going to, anyway. But then I walked in on him with Becca. She was my friend. Or at least I thought she was. They told me I was an idiot for thinking Lucky and I had ever been monogamous. Didn't I know he had been sleeping around this entire time?"

I shake my head and open my eyes, keeping my gaze on my lap.

"It was like he wanted me to catch them, as some sort of punishment for leaving modeling. And Becca . . . well I don't know why she did it. Maybe jealousy? Not that I had much to be jealous over. After that, I lost it. I went into a deep depression, wouldn't return any calls, not even from my family or Victoria. My sister had to fly out and drag me out of it. After a lot of talking with my family and with a therapist, I put myself back together and then started at the bottom. It was hard. I had to learn to forgive and move on. The forgiveness wasn't necessarily for Becca and Lucky, but for myself. Understanding that it's okay for me to make mistakes. Learning from them and moving on."

He's silent. I open my eyes and look over at him.

His thumb rubs against my wrist. "And now we're here."

"So we are. Sorry for all of that verbal spewage. Do you want to jump out of the car screaming yet?"

He laughs. "No. Not at all. I think it takes a lot of strength to come back from something like that, dealing with someone like Lucky. It makes me wish I had punched him when we ran into him."

"He's not worth it. But I have to admit. It's one of the reasons I've been so focused on my goal. It's like, if I can get someone to pick up my idea, I can prove to myself that he was wrong. I really am good enough. That I can do this."

"I think you already have." He glances over at me and our eyes connect. His hand squeezes mine and he returns his gaze to the road. "You said Marissa is still friends with him?"

"She befriends anyone and everyone who can get her information that sells magazines."

He scoffs. "I can't believe I dated her for two months."

"Two whole months, huh? How did you guys meet anyway?"

"At a charity event. She was there and she was so sincere and I fell for it. She didn't even care about the scars."

"Marc." I wait until he's looking at me. "Nobody cares about the scars but you."

"I know that's not true. Marissa did care. She just pretended she didn't."

"Okay, now I think she's a total psycho *and* a terrible person but how do you know she was pretending? Maybe she really didn't care."

"She never touched them, but that's nothing new. Most people avoid looking and touching. She was good at pretending, but she never got close."

"I've touched them." I have to laugh at myself. "I touched them and we barely knew each other."

He meets my eyes for a few long seconds. "I know."

His hand has been loosely gripping my wrist this entire time, but now he squeezes it once, gently, and removes it, turning his eyes back to the road.

Chapter Fifteen

The guy who takes a chance, who walks the line between the known and unknown, who is unafraid of failure, will succeed.
        –Gordon Parks

Marc

"Can you help me?"

"I'm not a shrink, Marc. I'm your IT girl." Charlie is sitting in the chair across from my desk. It's too high for her and she swings her legs like a kid.

"I'm not asking for mental help. What did you find?"

All of the company's legal documents are encrypted and I had Charlie hack into them to see if dear old Dad had made any changes since I last had my hands on them.

I had to do it the shady way because I didn't want him finding out.

It's the Monday after Thanksgiving. I spent the whole weekend working, and thinking. Thinking way too much. About Gwen, about how she was able to leave her emotionally abusive relationship with her ex, and yet I'm still in mine.

"I'm also not an attorney," she scolds me. "You know you could get me in trouble for all this snooping."

"Charlie, I promise I will take the heat if there is any. And there's no one else here I can talk to about this and trust that they won't run to Daddy and tell on me."

"From what I could find, everything is still the same and your dad has a hundred percent ownership interest."

"Not surprising." He likes to be in control of everything and everyone. "Is there anything in the contract about quitting?"

"The contract doesn't have anything about a time limit for employment. You can quit any time you want."

"Really?"

"That's good news, right?"

"It is." It means that I'm merely an employee. I have nothing to tie me here. Other than the money I make and what I've funneled into donations to the kids club. No to mention the people who work for my dad that I protect from his particular brand of crazy.

"You're thinking about everyone else again," Charlie says.

"How can I not?"

"It's okay to be selfish sometimes." She leans forward in the seat, her face earnest. "You do so much around here, but the world won't end if you aren't here."

"Ouch."

"Oh, don't even try to tell me it's an ego thing. What if you hire your own replacement before you leave? And don't tell your dad. Your job entitles you to hire and fire employees, right? There's nothing legally preventing you from quitting."

I lean back in my chair and stare at the ceiling. "Gwen said pretty much the same thing."

"Hot and smart. I love her."

I roll my eyes. "I could do it."

But then I still don't know what I want to do out there in the real world. If I do this, there's no coming back. I've always wanted to travel. Now's my chance. But what comes after that? I need more of a purpose than backpacking around the world like some teenager on a gap year. Don't I? Do I? I guess I don't need to work. Not really. My life has been nothing but slaving away for Dad and the company since I graduated from college. I could spend time enjoying my money instead of making it.

The thoughts are both thrilling and terrifying.

"You look like you might poop your pants."

I chuckle. "It's just . . . scary."

"Oh, come on, Marc. You're a trust-fund baby. You don't have to do anything."

It's an echo of my own thoughts. But I need something to give my life purpose, right?

Which makes me think of Gwen and her dreams and ambitions.

I would follow her around the world.

I shake away the thought. She's not mine to follow.

Two hours and a million tasks later, Dad strides into my office. "Marc, I need those marketing reports from yesterday."

I don't bother looking up at him. "I left them on your desk. Did you have a nice Thanksgiving?"

"Glory broke up with me."

That catches my attention. "I'm . . . sorry?"

"No you're not." He sits in the chair across from me. "The truth is that I'm not really sorry either."

This is so weird. Are we having a real conversation about something?

"You know, if your grandfather were still alive, he'd be proud of how hard you work."

I consider him, not really knowing how to respond. Does this mean he's proud of me but he's using my dead grandfather to try and pay me a compliment instead of telling me he's proud of me himself? Or is this some kind of veiled insult? My grandpa was kind of a dick. Kind of like Dad, actually. Business always came first.

Wait, am I another version of them?

"Anyway, do you have any friends that might like to date an older gentleman with lots of money?"

And we're back to being inappropriate. "No, Dad, I don't."

"I knew I should have asked Brent," he mutters before getting up and walking out.

I get back to work. I'm leaving early because I promised Brent I would meet up with him later.

Ever since Thanksgiving, I've been avoiding my brother. It's not hard to do since he's barely home anyway.

But this week he's on a bye and he's harassed me into playing a pick-up game of basketball, just like we used to.

I want to ask him about Gwen. He mentioned before Thanksgiving that he wouldn't mind if their relationship became more serious. Does he mean it? Does he want her? Is he going to pursue something?

There's no denying my own feelings anymore. Gwen and I have kept up a fairly steady stream of texts since I dropped her off the other day. I told her about what Charlie and I discussed, and she sent me a Morpheus meme that said, *What if I told you, you don't have to wait until New Years to make positive changes in your life?*

I sent one back with a little blonde girl in pigtails, her hands up, her expression confused. *My reaction when someone asks me what I want to do with my life.*

I can't worry about Brent, I just need to ask him. Then I can talk to Gwen and see if she feels the same. I know she wants to leave the city. I know she doesn't want a relationship. And maybe she'll reject me, but this is stupid. I'm a grown-up. I can have a grown-up conversation with my brother about his fake girlfriend.

We've been playing for thirty minutes before I build up the nerve. I'm dribbling the ball at half-court, Brent in front of me waiting to block when I finally speak. "I need to talk to you."

"I need to tell you something, too."

"You first." I fake to the left and dart to the right. The play works and I make my shot.

It bounces off the rim and Brent catches the rebound easily. "I think I'm going to ask Gwen to date me for real."

My heart is already pounding with exertion and it skips a few beats with his words. "Really?" I don't even try to steal the ball back. I stand there with my hands on my hips and my tongue stuck in a dry vise.

He shoots and the ball swishes through the net with ease. "Yeah. I really like her."

The ball is bouncing next to me. I grab it and hold it in front of me, like it will prevent the rest of me from falling into the black hole of this conversation. "When?"

"Tonight. We have a date." He eyes me speculatively. "You like her, right?"

Yes. And that's exactly the problem.

But I know that's not what he's asking. He doesn't think of it that way. He wouldn't. I'm his scarred older brother who takes care of things, and the only women that ever want me just want to get to him. I'm not the one that dates supermodels and actresses. Why would he ever think otherwise?

"She's a great girl," I finally say.

Brent grins his megawatt, million-dollar grin. "She is. I haven't felt this way about anyone since, well," he lifts his brows, "you know who."

Bella really effed him up. I would be so happy to see him happy with someone else. Anyone else.

And Gwen isn't mine to covet. She never has been.

Why does it suddenly feel like my chest has been poked with a thousand tiny needles?

"Do you think she'll be into it? I mean, does she act like she shares your feelings since this whole thing started?" Back at the half-court, I have the ball again. "She wants to leave New York, you know," I add. Out of desperation maybe, but I try to keep my tone light.

This time, I don't try to run the ball. I take a shot at half-court. It teeters on the rim before falling away.

I miss again.

He grabs up the ball as it bounces back toward us. "Yeah, but I travel a lot, too. And I have time in the off-season. I won't really know until I ask." He steps up to shoot and it swishes through the net.

He's so nonchalant. He has nothing to worry about. Of course she'll be into dating Brent. No woman in her right mind would turn him down. Well, except Bella. The thought gives me hope.

What am I thinking? I want my own brother to be happy, don't I?

"So. Tonight huh?"

"Yep. Well, I don't know. Maybe. I don't want to spook her. She's a little skittish."

More hope. She didn't seem that skittish to me. Not when I was kissing her in the Hamiltons' kitchen.

"Good luck, man."

He runs over and grabs the ball from where it's settled on the gym floor and passes it to me. "Your turn. What did you want to talk to me about?"

"Oh. It was nothing."

He frowns but doesn't press the issue. Then his face breaks into a smirk. "You cool to come out with us on Friday? I have a hot date for you."

I had nearly forgotten. Since it's a bye, a bunch of Brent's teammates plan on meeting up at some hot new club where they can sit in the VIP section and act like kings. Starlee suggested Brent and Gwen make an appearance, and Brent wanted me to come with them.

"Sure, that's fine." I take another shot from the top of the key and this time, the ball goes wide and curves next to the net. I'm not even close.

~*~

"How do I look?" Brent stands in the doorway of my office at home and adjusts the tie around his neck.

"Good."

"Yeah? I'm a little nervous. That's a first." He laughs.

"I'm sure it will all work out." What I'm actually thinking is *fuuuuuuuuuck*.

Brent looks good. I mean, he always looks good, but all dressed up and in a new suit, he looks like he stepped out of a magazine ad. Kind of like Gwen.

This sucks.

"Don't wait up. I'm taking her to the wine cellar at il Buco." He flashes me one last bright white flash of teeth and then disappears from the doorway. "I'll see you later, maybe," he calls.

He leaves, whistling.

I throw a paper clip from my desk onto the floor, watching it land with no sound or effect on anything at all.

I'd make a terrible diva.

How is he going to bring it up, the whole I-want-more thing? What is she going to say?

This isn't something I have control over. I need to divert my mind.

I spend an hour working on some reports and googling potential career changes. Then another hour watching TV, but nothing is derailing my thoughts and each hour feels like a full day.

What if she goes for it? Why wouldn't she go for it?

Because maybe she really likes you.

The little voice in my head is an idiot.

Finally, around eleven I go back to my room instead of waiting around in the living room. What if they come back here together? I don't want to see that.

When I finally hear the door click open after midnight, I listen intently.

Brent's feet move down the hall with gentle taps into his room.

There's only one set of steps.

He's alone. With that thought comes a surge of relief. Whatever happened tonight, she's not here with him. He's not at her place either. He's not removing her clothes or touching her body or kissing her the way I've been imagining for weeks.

Part of me wants to run into his room and jump on his bed and ask him what happened, but emulating a tween girl is a bit much, even for me.

There's no choice but to wait until morning to find out.

Which is why I sleep like shit.

I'm making extra-strong coffee the next morning when Brent comes out of his room, not looking much better than I feel.

He sits at the counter, hunched over his phone, hair rumpled, eyes tired, mouth slightly downturned.

"Coffee." I hand him the first cup with cream and sugar, just like he likes it, and then push the button to brew mine.

"Thanks," he murmurs and takes a sip, eyes still focused on his phone, clicking buttons.

I bite my tongue, waiting, waiting, waiting for him to say something.

It isn't until I'm drinking my own cup and checking my emails on my laptop, trying to ignore the urge to throw it at him, when he finally speaks.

"Do you think there's something wrong with me?"

I meet his eyes. He's more alert now, but there's still a pinch to his mouth and concern tightening his eyes. "What do you mean something wrong with you? I don't think there's anything wrong with you."

"It's just that," he runs a frustrated hand through his hair, "the women who want me, I don't want. And the ones I want, don't want me. At some point, it's not the world's fault these things always happen to me, it's mine, right?"

"Um." I lean back in the chair and remove my hands from the keyboard. "I take it things didn't go well with Gwen last night?"

"Yes. No. I don't know."

"That's perfectly clear."

"I . . . couldn't say the words. I know, it's stupid, but the signals she was sending were all wrong. So instead I made some moves. Subtle ones, you know, to see if she would reciprocate."

"And?"

He sighs and his lips press into a thin line. "I couldn't really tell. She's super nice, but I feel like . . . I've been friend-zoned."

I grimace. He's not happy. Inside, I have to squelch the lightness spreading into my chest.

Everything inside me is at war.

I don't want Brent to be unhappy, but if Gwen had returned his "moves," whatever those are, no doubt something gorgeous flirty people understand more than us mere mortals, it would have broken my heart. Shit. I don't want to be that guy, that jealous guy.

Outwardly I'm sure I could fake happiness, even if it did mean dying inside a little every day, but I'm so relieved, too.

I don't know what to say.

"I'm sorry, man."

He shrugs. "It is what it is."

"How much longer do you have to fake date her?"

"I don't know. I'll have to talk to Starlee. It might be a good idea to get some distance, but at the same time, I don't want to lose my chance. You know what I mean? And we've got that double date coming up, Friday night. You're still in, right?"

I nod.

"Maybe you can help me figure out what she's thinking. Or maybe you can ask her some questions, something, you know, indirect to find out if she has feelings for someone else maybe? Or to find out what she thinks of me?" He laughs and shakes his head. "I sound like a middle-schooler. Marc, you have to help me. Please?"

I swallow. What else can I say? "I will."

Chapter Sixteen

Only photograph what you love.
–Tim Walker

Gwen

"I showed the pictures to Warren and he loved them," Starlee says.

I hold in my urge to squee and jump around the room like a hooligan.

Because I'm a professional like that.

"That's so great," I say.

Before Thanksgiving, I called Starlee to tell her the issues I was having with getting her connections to listen to my pitch. She had me send her some of my endangered language pictures with the proposal for that piece. I also sent her an outline for the project I want to pursue abroad.

I've been on pins and needles for the last week, but she finally came through.

"He also said there might be interest in your idea at *News Weekly*, and he's going to put in a good word for you, if you're interested in making a presentation."

"Yes, absolutely!" It's my dream. It's what I've always wanted. It's what I've been working on for the last few years, and now it might actually happen.

"Great. They have you scheduled for next Monday. Bring your portfolio and a marketing plan."

The excitement of that win is dampened by my most recent date with Brent.

Thankfully, it's been a couple of days since I've seen him. Something was different. First we went to dinner at the wine cellar at il Buco, not exactly the best place for a prime photo op. I mean, it's in a freaking cellar. But Starlee wants us out more, acting like a couple in places Joe Schmoe and his camera phone can catch us rather than paparazzi, so I didn't think much of it. But then there was the walk afterward. He held my hand even inside the car and when he walked me to the door, he leaned. Again. This time wasn't like Thanksgiving, there was no getting around it. It was unmistakable.

That's what guys do, guys who want to see if you're interested. He stood in my doorway, watching my mouth, and he leaned.

I didn't lean back. I couldn't. I blurted a quick goodnight and slipped inside my apartment, shutting the door behind me.

What could this mean? We can't... I mean, he can't... So does that mean Brent is having more than friendly feelings for me? God, I hope not. This doesn't need to be any more complicated. I'm already falling for his brother. His beautiful, kind, selfless brother. And if Brent likes me and I like Marc and Marc likes... maybe me? I don't know. We did kiss, but then it was like nothing happened.

And I shouldn't be falling for anyone. I have goals that don't involve relationships.

I'm so fucked.

And I don't know what to do. I can't tell anyone the truth, but I *have* to talk to someone. If I've learned anything in the last year, it's that I need to reach out to someone when I need help. And I can't talk to Gemma. She'll freak and blow everything out of proportion.

That leaves my one friend in the city. Scarlett. We've hung out a few times since she had her cupcake meltdown in my living room. Plus we've been texting back and forth occasionally.

And there's nothing in the NDA to stop me from talking about Marc, even if I can't tell her the total truth about Brent.

So the day after my disaster date with Brent, I invite her over for takeout.

"How's the job hunt going?"

We're sitting on my futon in front of the TV, eating Chinese food and drinking martinis.

"It's not." She stabs the kung pao chicken with her fork. "And Mr. Guy I'm a Jerk Face Chapman has basically had me blackballed."

"What do you mean?"

"I applied for a couple of different dessert chef jobs at Per Se and Daniel and they looked at me a bit funny after I gave them my name. I thought maybe it was because of the article, you know, but I think he's told everyone about how I burned his jacket."

I grimace. "Oh no."

"Oh, yes." She stabs her fork into the container again. "I swear, chefs are the biggest jerks on the planet." She points her stabby fork in my direction. "Don't ever get involved with one. No matter how nice they seem or how good they can cook, they're all egotistical turds."

I hold my hands up in surrender. "I promise I will never date one. Do you want me to punch him in the balls?"

"Yes, actually."

"Maybe we can find his picture and print it out and throw things at it."

That makes her laugh. "That might be helpful, too. You're a good friend, Gwen."

I smile. "You're a good friend, too. I'm glad you brought me those cupcakes after that crazy night at Miguel's. You know, I don't . . . I don't really have many girlfriends."

"Well, most girls are probably intimidated by your looks. They don't want their men falling in love with you. If I had a man to worry about, I might run out of here, too." She smiles and I know she's kidding.

"You're not completely wrong. The only other friend I had since I moved to the city . . . well, let's just say that didn't end well."

"What happened?"

"I walked in on her with my boyfriend. They were both naked. And, you know."

"Holy fudge on a rocket."

"Yep. The worst part was that when I got upset, they acted like I was crazy. Like, why was I so upset? Didn't I know Lucky and I weren't exclusive? Didn't I know he slept with half the city? Even my supposed best friend, who knew how I felt about him, didn't seem to care. I haven't talked to her since that day."

"What a butt-nugget."

"Yeah, they both are that for sure. The weird thing is, even though Lucky was supposedly my boyfriend who I was in love with, the betrayal from Becca hurt my heart worse, I think."

We eat in silence for a few moments. Then Scarlett hands me my fortune cookie. "You need dessert."

"Thanks."

The wrapper crinkles as she opens hers, and then she holds it and peers at it. "You know, I bet if this Becca was a cookie, she'd be a whoreo."

I snort out a laugh. "You're probably right." We're quiet again, only the sound of her cookie crunching in her mouth and the TV. Then I say, "If she was an aquatic mammal, she'd be a whorca."

We both burst into laughter.

"If she made popcorn, she'd be Whorville Redenbacher!"

We laugh so hard for so long that my mouth starts hurting.

When we've calmed down and stopped the giggles long enough to eat our cookies, Scarlett says, "You know, I bet that makes it hard to trust people again. After being betrayed like that by the people you love."

"Yeah. It is."

"Well, just so you know, you can trust me. I won't tell anyone your secrets and I will never betray you. Mostly because I don't know anyone else, but also because I believe in doing the right thing, always. It's like Granny used to say, your word is only as good as your last meal."

I nod. "That makes perfect sense."

We talk a bit more about her latest audition and then I tell her what Starlee said and about my presentation scheduled at *News Weekly* next Monday.

"That's so amazing!"

And then I sneak out the real thing that's been on my mind all weekend.

"Also I might have kissed Marc on Thanksgiving," I mumble the words and immediately take a long drink of my dirty martini.

Scarlett stares at me for a few long seconds. "Isn't Marc Brent's brother? You made out with your boyfriend's brother?"

"Well when you put it like that . . ." I grimace. "It's not as bad as it sounds."

"How is that not as bad as it sounds?"

"For one, I've never really made out with Brent. At least, not unless it was in front of the press." I watch her, waiting for my words to sink in.

"You've only made out with Brent in front of cameras?"

"Yes."

Her head cocks to one side. "Are y'all pretending to date?"

"No," I say, while nodding my head yes.

"This is really confusing."

I groan and my head falls into my hand.

"Wait!"

I peek through my fingers at her.

She purses her lips for a second before speaking. "Are you and Brent together?"

I shake my head no. "Yes."

"Is this one of those things where you can't tell me the truth?"

"No." I nod my head yes.

"So you're pretending to date Brent, but you're falling for his brother?"

"No." I bob my head up and down.

She rolls her eyes.

I groan. "I'm in so much trouble."

"I guess so, since we can't even have a normal conversation about what's happening in your life right now. But it sounds complicated. What about your presentation on Monday? If that works out, then you won't be here long enough to have to deal with all this guy nonsense, right?"

"I know. And I would never give up my dreams for a guy. But . . . "

"But? You love Marc?"

"What? No. Uh-uh. Absolutely not. I don't know him well enough to assign an emotion of that weight to my feelings. But if I leave . . . I'll miss him. More than I'll miss Brent."

"What if he was willing to wait for you? Or join you?"

I bite my lip. "I can't ask that of him."

"Why not?"

"He . . . I don't know."

"You're scared."

"Yeah."

She puts a hand over mine. "Thanks for trusting me with your secret. I promise you won't find me naked with Marc. But you'd be okay if it was Brent, right?"

I laugh. "Yeah. That might actually be helpful."

Chapter Seventeen

I've never made any picture, good or bad, without paying for it in emotional turmoil.
    –W. Eugene Smith

Gwen

The only contact I have with Brent this week is via text. Just a few quick messages discussing particulars of our double date, where we are going (dinner and then 1 Oak), what time he's picking me up (eight o'clock), simple things that mean nothing.

I'm not sure who we're doubling with, but I imagine it's one of his teammates since that's who we're supposed to be meeting at the club.

Unlike Brent, Marc and I exchange texts and emails all week. We send funny memes and messages back and forth, plus he tells me about trying to leave the company. I tell him how proud I am of him. I know it's hard. I know it's scary, but he's a strong and capable person.

I'm ready at 7:55 when the buzzer rings from downstairs. "Coming down," I say into the speaker and then give myself one last once-over in the mirror on the door. I went with a simple black, strapless dress that stops just above the knee. Paired with strappy heels and chunky silver jewelry, it's elegant and classic.

Brent's waiting for me at the front door in a snappy black and white suit with a thin black tie. He looks great.

He greets me with a smile and a quick kiss to my cheek. I'm relieved he doesn't go for the mouth.

I ask how their last game went and follow him to the car, only half listening while he talks about their recent win and the opposing team's defensive maneuvering and blah blah blah.

I can see figures in the back seat. Brent opens the passenger door. I slide in and turn toward the back to say hello.

Except I'm not looking at one of Brent's teammates. I'm looking at Marc. And sitting next to him is a voluptuous, dark-haired goddess in a bright red, low-cut dress with a slit up the side exposing a lean thigh.

"Oh. Hello," I say. Once the words escape I realize they sound bitchy as fuck, so I temper my words with a bright smile.

"You must be Gwen. I'm Candy." She sticks out her hand.

I shake it, noting her firm grasp. "Nice to meet you," I murmur.

Brent's already made it to the driver's seat. "Candy is a cheerleader for the Sharks."

"That's great." My tone sounds dry even to myself.

This is ridiculous. Candy is probably a great person. The fact that she's obviously in this car as Marc's date is not lost on me and I'm being irrationally jealous. After all, I'm Brent's date. Even though we aren't really dating. And he's not mine to be jealous over. Besides, I'm sure Marc just met Candy tonight anyway.

Marc speaks up. "She also volunteers at the kids club sometimes."

Okay, maybe they have met before.

I bite my lip because all I can think to say is that's great, and since I've already said that I can't say it again.

It's no big deal. They're all friends.

Except they're in the back seat, together, murmuring to each other in low voices.

My stomach twists.

Jealousy, thy name is Gwen.

"You look beautiful tonight." Brent glances over at me with a grin and I force myself to smile back.

"Thank you."

This is going to be a long night.

~*~

Dinner is a nightmare. I mean, everything goes smoothly and I think I put on a good show, but inside I'm a squirming mess of misery.

Brent is solicitous and charming. He holds my hand and takes my coat and does everything a man should do on a date.

Candy is actually super nice and intelligent in addition to being super fit and gorgeous, so I only hate her more as the night goes on. Especially when she continually makes excuses to touch Marc on the arm and sits way too close to him and generally is in his vicinity more than I want to see anyone. Except myself.

Okay, so apparently that whole "I can make myself not like Marc" thing isn't working.

We finish eating dinner by ten and then it's time to head to the club. I wish I didn't have to go. I don't think I can stand watching Candy and Marc dance together as they do in these types of clubs, all sweaty bodies and pressed together and . . . just no.

I can't exactly say I want to go home because I can't stand watching Candy touch Marc all night, can I?

Should I plead illness? Headache? Yep, I absolutely should, but I do none of these things because I enjoy torture.

It's the only explanation.

When we pick up the car from the valet at the restaurant, somehow, I end up in the back seat with Marc and Candy is up front. By somehow, I mean when Candy talks about how much she loves Brent's Porsche and wishes she could drive it, I gently encourage the switch by getting into the back seat and stating loudly that she can have the next best thing by sitting up front on the way to the club.

Maybe it's obvious, but I almost don't even care. We chat on the way there about dinner, where we're heading, and then Candy and Brent talk about the other cheerleaders and football players that will be there. I kind of tune out. I'm too focused on Marc, sitting less than a foot away.

His hand is resting on the seat between us, and as an experiment, I lean slightly toward the middle seat, like I'm trying to hear the conversation between Brent and Candy. I rest my hand down next to his. Our pinkies are literally a centimeter apart.

For two long city blocks, I don't move.

We go over a bump and Marc leans slightly in my direction.

Another bump and I move my hand over, enough so that the skin of our pinkies are barely touching.

Then I hold my breath.

He doesn't move.

And then he does. With purpose. He lifts his pinkie and wraps it around mine.

My heart thumps in my chest, the tempo of my breath increasing. My stomach fills with heat. It's only an inch of skin connecting us, but I'm more turned on than I've ever been in my life. He's watching me, his eyes glittering in the darkness.

"We're here." Brent stops in front of the club, a celeb hotspot called 1 Oak, and then my door is opened and the connection is lost as we get out of the car and head past the line and inside.

The space is crushed with people. I catch a glimpse of a long, sleek black bar on one side. The flooring is checkered black and white, and giant chandeliers hang from the roof above us, not so much lighting the space as much as casting flecks of light into the darkness below. The air is full of a mixture of perfumes and aftershave combined with sweat and possibilities.

Brent grabs my hand and leads me through the crowd. Marc and Candy are somewhere behind us and I imagine Marc holding her hand as well. The thought makes me involuntarily squeeze Brent's fingers harder.

We stop near the back of the club where tables and chairs are reserved for VIPs. Some of Brent's teammates are there and they bump fists and clap backs. He introduces me to them but I can barely hear over the music.

I make small talk—as much as anyone can make when the bass is thumping and I can't hear the words coming out of my own mouth.

I try and focus on the other players, and not Marc and Candy who have joined the group, sort of. They're sitting at a couple of chairs in the corner, their heads leaned toward each other while they talk about something that looks important. Or intense. Or something.

In my head, they're discussing the best and quickest way to get out of here and rip off each other's clothes.

Ugh. I'm making myself sick. I can't stand here and try not to watch them.

"Let's dance." I grab Brent's hand and tug gently. He grins at me and then he steps way too close.

"Sounds great." His mouth is next to my ear.

What am I doing?

It's part of the show, a voice in my head insists.

Liar.

Before I can take it back, we're on the dance floor, pressed against each other, his hands on my waist and mine around his neck. It means nothing. We're not doing anything more than anyone else here is doing, in fact, some of these couples are grinding like they're about to orgasm right in the middle of the crowd. We're practically puritanical.

But I get the sense that Brent wants to kick it up a notch. He's not pushy or anything, but he leans down a little closer and runs his nose against the skin of my neck.

My breath catches, but not in a sexy way. I turn my back to Brent, still pressed against him dancing, and that's when I see them.

Candy and Marc have joined us on the dance floor. Her hands are all over him, running up and down his back. She leans closer and says something in his ear, their position not unlike the one Brent and I were just in.

But I want to puke. I'm the biggest hypocrite on the planet since Brent's hands are gripping my waist and pulling me back against him and I'm doing nothing to stop any of it.

I can't handle this. I am not this person.

I whip around, forcing his hands to fall off my body. "I have to go to the bathroom."

His eyes are concerned. "Are you okay?"

"Yeah. It's fine. I'll be right back." Without making eye contact I bolt for the ladies room.

It's kind of far away, at the back of the club, up a flight of stairs, and down a long, dark hallway.

And of course, there's a line. When all I want to do is hide in a stall and freak out for a minute, I can't even get that right. After a few minutes of standing around, it doesn't appear the line will be moving any time in the current century, so I finally give up and head farther down the hallway.

I need somewhere away from prying eyes so I can have a meltdown for a minute. Or twelve.

There's an unmarked door farther down and I open it. It's some kind of janitor closet. Just a narrow room with shelves of toilet paper and cleaning supplies. There's a small glow coming from a night-light on the wall.

Perfect. I step inside, a surge of relief waving through me. I turn to close myself inside, but Marc stops the door before I can shut it.

"Hey. Is everything okay?"

I press a hand to my chest. "Jesus."

"It's actually Marc, but I get that a lot."

"Haha. You scared me." I hit him gently in the shoulder with the back of my hand.

"You seemed a little weird downstairs."

"I'm surprised you noticed." I immediately regret the snarky tone in my voice. It's not fair.

"What is that supposed to mean?"

"Nothing. I'm sorry, I guess I don't feel well."

"Do you want me to take you home?"

Yes, that's exactly what I want, him to take me home and ravish me within an inch of my life. Maybe then I can get all these feelings out of my system. But I can't. We can't.

Wait, why can't we?

"No," I say. "Yes. I mean, Marc, I can't do this anymore."

"Do what anymore?"

I can't read his eyes in the dim light, but his tone is careful.

It's better that I can't see him well. It makes the truth easier to spill. "I can't keep pretending. Not since Thanksgiving. I know you think it was a mistake. But . . ."

He's not saying anything. He's so close, my rapid breathing pulls in the faint scent of his cologne. There's silence between us, along with the dulled thump of bass from downstairs and the constant pulse of unmet desires.

I lean toward him, putting a hand on his shoulder. In my heels, we're the same height so it's only too easy to press into him and set my mouth against his.

He tenses for a split second and then erupts into motion.

This is no soft meeting of bodies and lips. We're not in someone else's house while everyone is sleeping and we're stealing pie in the kitchen. We're completely alone. There's no reason to stay quiet.

One of his hands weaves into my hair, holding my head in place while his mouth ravages mine, full of the same pent-up emotion that's been killing me all night long, making me groan and grasp him tighter. His other hand is on my waist, pressing me back against the wall. The heat at my front is a stark contrast to the cold wall at my back. My hands grip his back, pulling him as close as possible while my lips meet his. Every frustration I've felt over the last few weeks adds to the hunger between us, making the rough clashing of our mouths a heady relief.

After an indeterminate amount of time, he pulls back and rests his forehead against mine.

Our labored breaths mingle in the air between us, along with a hefty dose of sexual tension.

"Gwen," his voice is tortured. "We can't."

"Why not?"

"My brother—" He stops, refusing to go on.

"Your brother and I are temporary. It's not real."

"Isn't it?"

"No."

I mean, Brent has *leaned* a couple of times, but I'm sure it meant nothing. He's lonely and wants some action. He doesn't *like* me. Not like this.

After a few more moments of standing there in the cramped space, catching our breath, he finally steps back.

I can see him erecting his walls in the glow of the night-light. His arms cross over his chest and he won't meet my eyes. "I'm—"

"If you say you're sorry," I step into his space, forcing him to look at me, "I will . . . do something highly irregular."

God, that was lame.

Ugh. I open the door and flee into the hallway, but of course he's right behind me.

"Gwen," he starts. I turn around, grab him by the tie and kiss him on the mouth, once, hard.

"Don't ever apologize to me like that again."

"I won't." His hands are lifted, placating.

I sigh and glance down the dark hall. There's still a line of people for the bathroom but none of them are paying attention to us. Not sure they could even see us from there.

A warm hand falls on my bare shoulder and I turn back to Marc.

"I'm not sorry," he says, and then his mouth falls on mine. Not hard and bruising this time, but soft and tempting. "I was never really sorry. I never thought it was a mistake. You could never be a mistake."

This time I pull back. "You should come over. Later. Tonight. After all of," I wave a hand, "this is over. Please."

He doesn't say anything, indecision warring in his eyes.

"*Please*." I whisper it against his lips, and then I pull back for good and walk away, leaving him there alone.

Chapter Eighteen

Passion is in all great searches and is necessary to all creative endeavors.
    –W. Eugene Smith

Marc

I shouldn't be here.

Standing in her building, staring at her door. She buzzed me up a minute ago and now . . .

It's the only place in the world I want to be.

Well, second place, since she's on the other side.

There's a little sign flashing in my head. Abort, abort, bad decision.

Brent's the one that brought her home. By the time I made it back down to the first floor of the club after our little moment in the closet, they were gone.

Brent texted me that he left the car for me to take Candy home and then he took Gwen home in an Uber.

Very considerate of him.

And yet here I am. I drove his car here. After dropping Candy off at her place.

I'm sure he thinks I went home with her. That was his intention. She wasn't averse either, but she's not Gwen. She doesn't make my palms sweat or my heart skip a beat every time she smiles.

There's only one woman on my mind, and she's on the other side of the door.

I take a deep breath, thinking about tonight, everything that happened from our interlocked fingers in the car, to her dancing at the club with Brent, to our time in the janitor closet. My emotions surge all over again, from elation to jealousy and anger to pure joy.

I shouldn't be here. I should leave. Now.

If we get caught . . . it could ruin everything. Brent's career, the family business, my own relationship with my brother, who's only the most important person in my life.

But then the door swings open and there she is.

She's wearing a cropped T-shirt and boy-short-style underwear, looking like she just stepped out of a Victoria's Secret catalogue.

A groan escapes my throat.

How is it possible that the smile spreading her lips is for me? That glow in her eyes? She grabs my hand and yanks me inside and all thoughts of Brent and right and wrong fly away with one touch of her skin.

I barely notice the door shutting behind us even as she fumbles at the lock. I'm too busy pulling her shirt off, and then yanking her back against me. I want to feel her skin everywhere, all over me, against me, around me.

It's not enough.

It only takes a few seconds of tugging at her little shorts, then I'm lifting her and her long slender legs are around my waist. I press her against the wall and I'm still wearing way too many clothes.

There's only a few steps from the entryway through the miniscule kitchen and to the futon. I carry her there, still kissing, her hands in my hair and my hands holding her up and against me. I run into her side table but it doesn't matter because her couch is already folded down and I set her on it and then we're scrambling to remove the remaining layers between us. Nothing else matters, not the room, not the surroundings, just her. And me. Us.

She's unbuttoning my pants.

I'm yanking off my shirt.

And then there's nothing between our hot skin except our gasping breaths in the quiet air.

I rest between her spread legs. My erection is against her cleft but I'm not moving. Not yet. Our rough and tumble movements have slowed into something else, something infinitely more gentle.

We stare at each other, taking in the moment.

"You're so beautiful," she whispers, her fingers tracing a path over my face.

"That's my line." I turn my head and kiss her palm.

Her lopsided smile moves closer and then she's pressing her warm, sweet mouth against my scars and the tenderness of the touch makes me want to cry.

"Gwen," my voice breaks.

"I want you inside me," she whispers against my mouth.

The words break the temporary softness between us and I lean over, scrambling for my pants, looking for the condom I found in Brent's glove box before coming upstairs. She takes it from me, ripping the package with her teeth. I pull myself up slightly so she can reach down and roll it onto my length. The slow and delicate movements of her hand are making me lose my goddamn mind but I bite my lip and bear it.

And then she's tugging on me, pulling me closer again.

I slide into her slowly, taking my time, wanting to remember this moment and this feeling long after she's gone.

Once I'm fully seated, I stop and rest for a second. I have to take this slow and make sure she enjoys it.

What if this is it?

"Are you okay?" she asks.

"No." I drop my head on her shoulder. "You feel too good."

She laughs, the sound warm and the puff of her breath gentle against my ear.

"You feel better," she whispers. She tugs on my head, pulling me away from her shoulder and gripping the sides of my face until we're looking into each other's eyes. "I want to see you."

My eyes search hers, seeking the truth I know is there. She wants me. *Me*. She wants to know it's me moving inside her.

My thrusts are gentle and my heart is full as I watch her pupils dilate and a flush move up her chest.

Time ceases to exist as I move inside her, slow, and then faster.

I watch her squirm underneath me, paying close attention to her breathing, the flutter of her eyelashes, the way she bites her lip and moans. Taking her cues, I shift angles to hit her in exactly the right spot. Her breath comes out in pants, her back arches as she climaxes, and I think I've never seen anything so amazing in my life.

"Marc." Her voice is like her smell, like honey and sunshine, and the way she says my name as she comes pushes me over the edge. My own body erupts in pleasurable waves that leave me drained and more relaxed than I think I've ever been in my life. I sort of black out for a minute and when I come to, Gwen is running her nails up and down my back.

I'm still inside her.

"Am I crushing you?" I lift up but she pulls me back down.

"I like it when you crush me."

"Well in that case." I go limp on top of her, the sudden force of my weight eliciting a small scream and then a giggle.

180

I laugh, and her chest moves against mine as she joins in the chuckles. Her nipples are hard against me and I sit up a little so I can appreciate the sight. "You're so perfect." I whisper the words.

"No, you are."

I lean down again and kiss one of her breasts, flicking my tongue against her areola.

She gasps and my shaft begins hardening inside her.

"Again?" she breathes.

"With you? Always."

~*~

Sunlight wakes me, coming through a crack in the dark curtains and nailing me right in the eye.

For a second, I forget where I am, but then I suck in a breath that tastes like honey and sunshine and a warm hand snakes down between my legs and grips my erection.

"Good morning." Gwen's hair is a rumpled mess. She looks like she's been thoroughly fucked.

I grin at her, knowing I can't possibly look half as enticing as she does right now, but that isn't stopping her hand from wandering between my legs.

I groan.

"It's my turn," she says. She fumbles in a drawer next to the futon and pulls out a condom. Thank God she had extras. All I had was the one I stole from Brent's car and we've gone through more than a few, in between dozing off and on all night.

She covers my cock with the rubber and then she's sitting on top of me and I lose all thoughts for a good twenty minutes until she's the one lying on top of me, all dead weight and delicious, curvy, long limbs. I run my hands up and down her thighs. I don't think I could ever get enough of this and the thought is both glorious and terrifying.

My mind pokes at me. It wants to think about the future, and about Brent, about how he might feel about last night, but I purposefully shove the thoughts away.

"Shower?" Gwen says.

"And breakfast?" I add.

"It's like you're reading my mind."

The shower takes longer than it should because Gwen all wet and soapy is a dream that I don't want to wake up from. Gwen shares in the fun, enjoying the moment and not bringing up the future. Or the fact that we're hiding from the real world. I just want to hang on to whatever is between us for a little bit longer. At least for the rest of the weekend.

After our shower, we're in the small bathroom together. She's given me a spare toothbrush and I'm brushing my teeth while she's blotting her long hair with a towel.

She stops drying her hair and turns toward me, biting her lip. Thoughts swirl behind her eyes. "I wish we could go somewhere today. Do something together, in public. Go to breakfast? There's nothing to make here but . . ."

I spit out the toothpaste into the sink, my mind whirring with possibilities. I know what she's really saying. Where can we go where we can be ourselves and not be noticed? Where can we nurture this new and tender thing growing between us without prying eyes?

Nowhere in the city is completely safe.

"I have Brent's Porsche," I say, thinking. And then it hits me. "I have an idea. But we'll have to grab something to eat on the way."

"What are you thinking?"

I smile. "It's a surprise. Pack an overnight bag, and dress warm."

She squeals and hugs me before running out of the bathroom. I'm a little distracted by her exit because, well, she's completely naked and it takes me a minute to shake myself out of my stupor.

It's only the work of a few phone calls to set everything up.

Brent has a practice bag in his trunk with some clean jeans and a long-sleeved shirt. He's bigger than me, especially in the chest and arms, but the pants mostly fit except for being on the long side. I'm thankful I don't have to stop home and grab my own clothes and risk running into him. Which turns my thoughts to the only thing that could ruin my high from the last twenty-four hours.

Brent.

My brother.

My brother who told me that he's falling for his fake girlfriend. The same woman I've had over me, under me, around me so many times now that I've lost count.

Guilt threatens to choke me, but that doesn't stop the thoughts.

My brother who never took advantage of the fact that my past girlfriends would continually throw themselves at him.

But they weren't Gwen.

He didn't have . . . this. This insatiable need for someone.

I should tell Gwen about Brent and Brent about Gwen and then . . . and then what?

I can't let her go. Not yet.

All thoughts of Brent and what a terrible brother I am get shoved to the side. I'm going to enjoy this time while it lasts. Because it can't last. Can it?

While Gwen is getting dressed, I run to the bodega on the corner and grab a couple of breakfast burritos. There's a middle-aged woman at the counter with kind eyes, and I remember what Gwen told me about how she would have starved if it weren't for Maria at the bodega.

I leave a large tip before heading back to Gwen's.

She's ready when I get there and we waste no time.

"Are you going to tell me where we're going?" She's got her hair pulled back in funky pigtails and she's wearing jeans and boots and a sweater. She's sitting cross-legged in the passenger seat looking like the most delectable thing I've ever seen, even with the salsa on her lip.

"Nope. And there's rules."

"Rules? What kind of rules? Naked rules?"

My brows lift. "You want some naked rules?"

She taps a finger against her mouth, like she's seriously considering her reply. "Maybe."

"We can put those on the table." I stop at a light and take the moment to turn and cup her face, tilting her head toward mine to flick the salsa from the corner of her mouth with my tongue.

When I pull back, her eyes are shut and her mouth is open slightly. She shakes herself and then blinks at me. "Definitely need some naked rules."

I smile. "The other rule is no cell phones." I hold my phone up and shake it. "Mine's off." I toss it in the back seat.

"I can get behind that." She pulls her phone out of her purse and powers it down before throwing it in the

184

back with mine. "I have a rule, too. I get to take your picture as much as I want."

I grimace. "As long as you don't show them to anyone else. Ever."

"Ugh, you're so annoying. But fine. I don't mind keeping them all to myself."

Once we're out of the city, I link her hand in mine, relishing the feel of her slim fingers in mine.

I want to remember this moment forever.

Chapter Nineteen

The best lesson I was given is that all of life teaches, especially if we have that expectation.
–Sam Abell

Gwen

It doesn't take long to figure out where Marc is taking me, but I don't say anything, enjoying the comfortable silence between us interspersed with casual touches and the snap of my camera.

I take pictures of him driving, smiling, kissing my fingers. I want to capture these moments and hold them close. Something to remember later when . . .

I'm not thinking about that.

The future is for tomorrow. Today is about me and Marc.

The Hamptons are quiet in the winter. The streets are nearly empty. We drive past dried-up fields and bare trees, through small towns full of clapboard houses and buttoned-up buildings. We go all the way to the end of Long Island—as far east as you can get without driving into the ocean—and end up in Montauk.

As he winds the car into a neighborhood, I catch glimpses of the empty beaches. It's too cold to swim, but I still want to walk along the beach with him, even if I freeze.

He pulls up in front of a two-story grey clapboard house that backs up to the beach.

We park in the small driveway. A set of wooden stairs leads down from the front porch and disappears around back.

"We're here." He grins at me and then slides out of the car, opening the back door to pull out our bags. I get out and breathe in the crisp, salty air, stretching before following him up the stairs.

The front door opens into a long, open room. A couple of chairs and a small couch cluster around a fireplace and above it a flat screen on the wall. A dining set with a glass-topped table and bench seats nestles between the seating area and the kitchen, which is lined with stainless steel appliances, white cupboards, and a butcher-top island. In countless shell- and pebble-adorned photo frames, children romp and laugh in the sand.

Everything is clean and high quality, but instead of being sterile, the pictures clustered on the side tables in the living room and arranged on the walls give everything a homey, lived-in feel despite the fact that no one lives here full-time. A sliding glass door in the kitchen leads to the backyard. Next to the front door, a staircase leads up to the bedrooms, or so I assume.

"This is nice," I say.

"Mom bought it when we were kids. We used to come here in the summer." He tosses our bags on the couch and then walks into the kitchen. "Are you hungry?" he asks, opening the fridge. "We have a guy that maintains the property in the winter. I had him stock it with all kinds of stuff because I didn't know what you might be craving."

"I am hungry." Something in my voice must register with him because he steps back from the fridge and lets the door fall shut, his eyes meeting mine.

I walk over and grab the bottom of his shirt, pulling it over his head and tossing it onto the floor. "Have you ever had sex with anyone here?"

His throat jerks as he swallows. "No. I've never brought a woman here."

"Good."

We christen the kitchen island. Then a chair in the living room. Then the bench seat in the dining room.

Once that's been taken care of, we've worked off all the calories from the burritos and it's after lunchtime.

"Let's go out to eat," he says.

"Didn't you say you had a bunch of food here?"

"I know but I want to take you out."

"I won't argue with that."

We go to an Italian restaurant on the beach in Montauk, Harvest on Fort Pond. There's only one other couple in the restaurant and they look over eighty. Well, we are eating dinner at four thirty.

We hold hands and talk and eat pancetta roast shrimp and penne pasta, like lovers.

We take a couple of slices of apple blueberry pie to go.

Then we head back to the house and walk along the beach as the sun sets. I take more pictures. Marc in front of the tumultuous waves, in a sweater with windblown hair, while he laughs at something I've said. Marc gazing into the distance as we watch the sun escape under the waves. Marc watching me take his pictures with a rueful grin that turns into a grimace. Marc sticking out his tongue when I won't stop taking his picture. Marc coming after me and picking me up, tossing me over his shoulder and running with me down the beach.

188

Okay, well, I get pictures of the sand under his feet and some shots of his butt when he's carrying me like that, and they're terrible shots because he's jostling me around too much, and yet they might be my favorites.

When we get back to the house, frozen and windblown, he makes a fire and we sit in front of it. I show him some of the pictures I've been taking, wanting him to see what I see.

"Look." I click the button to give him the slide show, and when he's seen all of them, his eyes flick to mine.

"You're a talented photographer. Those are probably the best pictures I've ever been in. I look nearly normal."

I smack him on the leg. "Stop that. It's not because I took the picture, it's you. I'm only the link. It's not who takes the picture, it's who's *in* the picture. Photography is about making a connection to people. It's empathy. It's . . ." I try to put it into words, the way I feel about taking pictures of people. Of real moments and emotions. "The best part of photography is capturing a moment of humanity and freezing it forever. To be honest, I don't even see your scars anymore. Just you. And you are beautiful."

He shakes his head. "You almost have me believing it." He takes the camera from me with gentle fingers and puts it on the coffee table. "About those naked rules."

My smile is as big as the Atlantic. "I've never made love in front of a fire."

"That's something we need to fix."

~*~

189

The next morning is subdued. He makes me breakfast. It's nothing fancy, scrambled eggs and cut-up fruit, a bagel and cream cheese. He even makes some sandwiches to bring with us on our way back to the city. It's the little considerate things he does that makes my heart hurt. When I rub the goose bumps from my arms, he gets me my sweater from the living room. When I've finished my glass of juice, he asks if I want more.

He's always looking out for what I might need or want.

He's Marc.

The drive home is quiet. Not as exciting as the way out to Montauk. We're both bracing ourselves, I think, for reality to return.

He's going back to work tomorrow. He's going to talk to his dad about quitting. I have my presentation and if all goes well, I'll be leaving the city in the near future. Maybe for good.

All I've wanted over the past year is to leave and now I'm not ready for it to end.

We're still somewhere on Long Island when I unbuckle my seat belt and lean over Marc in the driver's seat.

"What are you doing?" he asks.

I answer by unzipping his fly.

"You don't have to . . . dear God."

I lift my head. "No, actually it's Gwen, but I get that a lot."

His chuckle turns into a moan when I once again drop my head, and then the rumble of the engine drops as he pulls over to the side of the road.

Thank God for tinted windows.

There's nothing more exciting than the sound of his moans and the feel of his fingers in my hair, gently encouraging. "Gwen, I can't," he pants.

I sit back and then pull off my leggings, keeping my eyes on his.

He pushes a button and the drivers seat moves back.

I take a few seconds of fumbling in my purse to find a condom and slide it on. Then I'm straddling him, feeling him stretch inside me, his eyes on mine, seeking, before he kisses me on the mouth, then his lips trail down my neck and I arch against him.

My body is sore from all the lovemaking, but I don't even care. It feels too good, too right.

His hips pulse upward, and we're frantic, both of us clinging to something we know won't last. I finally climax on a sob. His cock flexes inside me, coming moments after I've finished.

I collapse against him.

We don't say anything.

Our foreheads touch as we breathe together and I enjoy the feel of him inside me, ignoring the damn steering wheel digging into my back until I can't anymore. Then I slide back over to the passenger seat and pull on my leggings and buckle my seat belt. He's moving next to me, righting the seat, disposing of the condom and zipping up his pants, but I don't look over.

I can't. Not until he's parked in front of my building.

I gaze out the window for a second before turning to face him.

He's watching me. "I should walk you up."

"No. Don't."

"Can I see you tomorrow?"

"I don't know."

"This doesn't feel right."

I feel it, too, but still I ask, "What doesn't feel right?"

"Leaving you."

I lean toward him and our mouths meet over the center console. His hands sneak into my hair and I brace myself against his chest for a moment before pulling back. "I have to go."

He opens his mouth like he wants to say more, but then he nods.

I slide out of the car and shut the door. I grab my bag and phone from the back seat and then I'm jogging away.

I don't look back.

~*~

Once I'm alone in my apartment with nothing more than my thoughts and the scent of Marc's skin on my clothes and on my sheets, the panic sets in.

I pick up the phone to text him, then put it back down.

A minute later, I repeat the motion.

I want to call him to tell him Martha came over and stole my saltshaker. Or how nervous I am about my presentation tomorrow, even though I've been practicing it for years. Or even something gross, like how I found a piece of bread from our sandwiches in my cleavage a minute ago.

I want to talk to him about everything. Stupid things, funny things, things that don't matter, and things that do. I know I can say anything, be completely myself and he won't judge and he'll support me.

Holy shit.

I love him.

I can't. It's been, what, like three weeks? This isn't possible. I'm hormonal. I've been watching too many chick flicks.

What am I supposed to do now?

It's either cry or drink heavily, and since I have an important presentation tomorrow and I don't want to be red-eyed from either, I have to go with a third option.

"I can't come over." Scarlett calls me back after I send her a text. Her voice is a bit higher pitched than normal and she's breathing fast.

"Are you okay?"

"No. I'm baking."

"I thought you loved baking."

"I do. But I'm probably never going to be able to do it professionally. Ever." She sniffs.

"Don't panic. I'm coming over."

Scarlett doesn't live far from me, a small one bedroom in Washington Heights.

She lets me in and immediately returns to the counter to stir something in a giant bowl.

It's an open floor plan, which is a good thing because she's set up tables to extend her counter space from the kitchen into the living room. Counter space that is now covered in mixers, baking pans of various shapes and sizes, bags of flour, spices, and other accouterments.

She's moving like a dancer, stirring and measuring and doing whatever it is that chefs do.

"Try these." She shoves a small plate in my direction full of different finger-food desserts. There are chocolate-covered toffee bites, mini cupcakes, and some kind of fruity wonton-wrapped creamy thing that melts in my mouth and makes me groan out loud.

"This is really good," I say through my mouth of food.

"Are you sure?"

"I wouldn't lie. Do you have any more of these little wonton things?"

"Yes. Here." She gives me another plate and then takes a rag from her shoulder and tosses it on the counter.

"Are you okay?"

"Yes. No. I don't know."

I pop another dessert in my mouth and watch her carefully. "Do you want to talk about it?"

"You know why I went out with asshole Jerry? And all those other guys who never bothered calling me back?"

"Is this a trick question?"

"It's because I slept with my boss back in Blue Falls. He turned out to be married."

"Yikes."

"Right? I didn't know, by the way. Well, I knew he had been married, but he told me they were separated and going through a divorce. They weren't. He was a chef. We had a passionate, torrid affair, and when I learned the truth, I was devastated." Her stirring pace increases. "That's why when I got to New York and was ready to put myself out there again, I only picked guys on Grindr that didn't really do it for me . . . you know, *sexually*," she whispers the word, "and they were all *serious businessmen*. And do you know why?"

"Um, because you really like douchey guys that are only moderately attractive?"

"Because I don't want to end up in a relationship like my parents. Or like the one I had with Bruce."

"Bruce is the married chef guy?" I clarify.

She nods.

"I thought you said your parents are super in love and into each other."

"They are. And that's the problem. They are so passionate, to the absolute exclusion of everything and everyone else. Including their daughters. My relationship with Bruce was like that. I forgot about my dreams, and he forgot about the wife he had at home."

I nod. "So you want someone who doesn't make you feel too much. I don't think you need Grindr. I think you need a therapist."

She switches from stirring to chopping strawberries. "I don't need a therapist, I need someone I have lukewarm feelings for." The knife clicks down on the cutting board with swift, hard thrusts.

"That sounds like a horrible idea and why are you getting all worked up?"

She stops chopping and stares down at her mess of berries. "I lost my job today."

"Scarlett! What happened?" I rush over and put a hand on her shoulder.

She turns to face me. "One of our drunk customers asked to see the chef, and the boss always makes us go out and talk to them. The customer is always right!" She rolls her eyes. "Anyway, he was an older guy and he was dressed in a Santa costume. He said his burger was overcooked and when I reminded him that he asked for well done, he pointed at his crotch and told me I could crawl under the table and be his ho-ho-ho. So I dumped a chocolate shake on his head."

"Scarlett, I'm sorry."

"Me, too."

"So explain to me what losing your job has to do with you dating those asshats? You're not going out with horny Santa, right?"

"Yuck, no. But now I'm going to end up back in Blue Falls and I won't be able to get a job there either because Bruce owns every restaurant in town! What am I going to do, Gwen?"

"Why don't you work for yourself?"

195

She blinks at me. "I don't have the money to lease space in the city and start my own place. There's no way a bank would front that kind of money to an unknown chef."

"Not a restaurant. You've got a lot of desserts right here. What if instead of leasing a space, you do a dessert food truck or catering or something."

She stares at me.

"I can help you market," I add. "And I bet Brent would, too. Maybe he could tweet or something about how divine your desserts are to get some interest. Plus, I bet Liz would run a follow-up article, to show where you are now and what you're doing. It could be amazing."

She drops her spoon in her batter and throws her arms around me. "Gwen. That's a brilliant idea!" She pulls back, her hands still on my shoulders. "I'll have a lot to figure out, but it's just crazy enough to work. A dessert food truck," she mutters, then turns back to her mixing. "Okay, my crazy is all tapped out. It's your turn. Tell me something going on with you."

I bite my lip and then decide to just spill it. Why not? "I'm in love with Marc."

She stops stirring and cocks her head toward me. "The brother?"

"Yeah."

She shrugs a shoulder. "I kind of figured."

"You did?"

"Well, sure. I mean, Brent is the most handsome guy in the city. If you don't want to truss him up and bring him home, then it must be love."

"But now I don't know what to do."

"About what?"

"About my job. About his brother. About his issues and my issues and, and . . ."

"Honey, we all have issues. Did you not just hear what I said about wanting someone I don't really want too much? There's no reason you can't have issues and still be together. And why can't you have the job and the guy, too? There's no rule against it."

"It's not that simple."

"Maybe it is."

"If *News Weekly* likes my presentation, I might leave the country."

"That's a big deal," Scarlett agrees. "But he could go with you. Or he could wait for you. Have you even asked him?"

"No." I'm like a sullen, angsty teen. I should go hang out with Janice.

"Do you even have this job yet?"

I sigh. "No. You're right. I'm going to tell him."

I want to call him. I want to be with him. I'm going to do it, after my presentation tomorrow. But something feels off, and I don't know what it is. It's like there's a dark figure looming over me, waiting to drop the hammer.

Chapter Twenty

Character, like a photograph, develops in darkness.

   –Yousuf Karsh

Gwen

My presentation isn't until one, but I'm up early to prepare Monday morning. I brew coffee and get to work. I've been over this a million times, but there's got to be a way to make it better, to make it even more compelling, to get my words across.

There's a knock at my door and I get up to let Martha in.

"Hey, Martha. You want coffee?"

"Oh, yes, sweetie." She comes in slowly, shutting the door behind her, and I get out a mug and put it next to the coffee pot for her.

I get back to work, the sounds of Martha toddling around in my kitchen a familiar accompaniment. Which is why I barely hear when she asks me a question.

"What did you say?"

"The people calling me about you. I told them you're a nice girl who didn't do anything wrong."

"People . . . called you about me?"

"Yes, this morning."

What? I hadn't looked at anything online yet today. I shut the Wi-Fi off on my computer and kept my phone off so I wouldn't be distracted. I turn it back on and, with a sinking feeling of doom, load up my web browser.

There's another article. In *Stylz*. Of course.

It's Marc and I.

My stomach drops when I see the pictures.

There's a fuzzy one of us kissing at the club the other night. Another clearer shot of him getting out of Brent's car and walking up to my apartment building. And yet another, both of us in Brent's car, driving away the next morning, clearly freshly showered and smiling and . . . oh God.

This is a disaster. This is going to ruin Brent's career. No one will believe anything he says. This will kill him. And Marc and their family business. Their dad is going to freak out and Marc will end up dealing with most of the fallout. Not to mention my interview later today . . .

With shaking hands, I turn on my cell phone. There's a ton of missed calls, but none of them are Marc. He hasn't seen the article yet.

I glance over the story again, seething when I notice the title. "Beauty and the Beast." Fucking Marissa.

I call Marc.

"Hey, beautiful," he answers after one ring, his voice light and happy.

"Marc." My voice cracks on his name.

"What's wrong?"

"I . . . you haven't seen it."

"Seen what?"

"There's . . ." I can't say it. Instead, I sigh and say the one word I know will clue him in. "Marissa."

He's already clicking away, the tapping of his fingers the only sound until— "Shit."

There's a click and the line goes dead. I stare at my phone. Did he hang up on me? I try to call and it goes straight to voicemail.

No, he doesn't get to do this.

I grab my keys and purse and then I'm out the door, walking in the direction of their apartment while tapping for an Uber on my phone.

It's takes forty-five minutes to drive to his place because of an accident on Henry Hudson Parkway. I want to scream, but that won't make the cars in front of us move any faster.

The doorman recognizes me and lets me go up.

I have to talk to him. See him. I want to throttle Marissa when I think of the pain she's already put him through, and now this?

I knock, frantic, and the door swings open and there he is, in slacks and a button-up shirt like he was getting ready for work when I called. I want to rush into his arms but he's on the phone. He steps back to let me in.

"Yeah, she's here." He hands me the phone.

Confused, I take it. "Hello?"

"The presentation is off." It's Starlee.

My eyes fly to Marc's and I swallow past the lump in my throat and nod, even though she can't see me. I didn't even think about my appointment later today, or how this news would affect my deal with Starlee.

"What were you guys *thinking*? You were supposed to help Brent, not make things worse."

"I didn't . . . we didn't . . ."

"I don't have time for excuses. I'm too busy trying to fix your fuckup. No one in this town is going to give you a shot now, and you have no one to thank but yourself."

She hangs up.

I pull the phone from my ear and stare down at it, numb with shock. Starlee has the connections to ruin me. Completely. This is worse than what happened last year with Lucky and Marissa. I can't dig myself out of this. My dream is dead.

Marc takes it from me, careful not to touch my fingers with his.

The lack of contact chips off a piece of my heart. I step closer, as if the proximity will make him stop pulling away. "Marc, I'm sorry."

He shakes his head. "It's not your fault, Gwen, it's mine."

I don't have a chance to respond because the door swings open and slams against the wall, startling me into a jump.

It's Brent. When he sees us, standing next to each other in the doorway, he doesn't say anything. His eyes are trained on Marc, unblinkingly hostile. His jaw is tense, his arms rigid by his side.

Brent stalks past us into the living room and Marc follows him.

I follow Marc.

"Brent, listen," Marc starts.

"No, you listen. I never did that to you. Never. Not once. Not even when your girlfriends were throwing themselves at me, fully naked. I still kept my damn hands to myself."

"You weren't really dating!"

"Does it matter?"

I feel like an interloper, watching them fight, even though it is about me.

"You barely even know her."

"And you do?"

"Yes! I was the one spending time with her when you weren't here."

"I know, and I trusted you. More fool me. You *knew* I had feelings for Gwen," Brent says.

I'm stunned by that revelation. I mean, with all the leaning, I had an inkling Brent was wanting more than the fake dating, but I didn't think it was serious. I thought he just wanted to fool around or something, not that there were feelings involved.

We had fun, but everything we talked about was on the surface. It was never like with Marc.

"Oh, come on. This isn't about your feelings for Gwen, it's about how this is the first time a girl has chosen me over you and your ego can't take it." He smiles, but it's not any smile I've ever seen on Marc's face, filled with an almost ferocious glee.

It stuns me. Has it been about this the whole time?

"You have feelings for me?" I ask Brent. He nods and I turn to Marc. "Did you use me to serve your own insecurities about your brother?"

He blinks and his head moves back as if I've lobbed a direct hit. "No. You know I wouldn't do that."

Do I? Am I so damaged from Lucky and this damn city that I can't tell the difference between truth and fiction? A flood of panic threatens to overwhelm me. Everything I wanted was in reach. This is about so much more than Marc and Brent's issues. Things were changing for me, someone was going to take me seriously, and now . . . everything is ruined.

"I'm not sure what I know."

"Gwen," they both say.

I look at Marc—pleading and contrite—and then Brent—hurt and angry. And then I think about what I've lost today. It's too much. "I can't deal with this."

My feet are moving. They continue arguing behind me, but I keep walking in a daze into the elevator and out onto the street.

People walk by, on their cell phones, talking to each other, focused on getting to their lunch or work or whatever. I stand in front of Marc and Brent's building for a few minutes until the doorman asks if I want a cab. I wave him off and start walking.

I end up in Central Park by the Bethesda Fountain. It's cold and cloudy and people bustle by, hugging their jackets to themselves, trying to keep warm.

I don't have a sweater.

I don't want to be here anymore. I need my family. They always pick up my pieces.

Reaching into my purse, I find my phone.

My fingers are almost too frozen to swipe, but after a few tries the call connects. "Gemma?"

"Are you okay?"

Only one word from my mouth and she knows something is wrong.

The tears start to fall, warm tracks on cold cheeks.

"Gwen. What the hell is going on? Do I need to kill someone?"

"I don't know, Gemma. I thought he was ... I thought it was— I thought we were— I lost everything! Again!" And with that I burst into sobs.

It takes a few minutes for me to calm down. Gemma's talking, and I think it's mostly gibberish at first, just words in a soothing tone, but then she says, "Can you get to the airport?" in a sharp pitch that gets my attention and stops the waterworks for a minute.

My head drops forward. I have my wallet and phone. That's all I really need. "Yes."

"Get to JFK. Sam's booking you a flight out."

Home.

The thought sparks a little bit of warmth in the hole in my chest.

I'm going home.

Chapter Twenty-One

Love involves a peculiar, unfathomable combination of understanding and misunderstanding.
   –Diane Arbus

Gwen

By the time I touch down at the Reno-Tahoe International Airport, it's dark outside. It's only seven, though. I gained three hours on the five-hour flight from New York.

Sam and Gemma are waiting for me in the main terminal. I don't have any luggage, just my purse, so after a hug, we bypass baggage claim and they walk with me in between them to the car.

They don't ask questions or expect anything from me. They hustle me into the back seat, speaking in quiet voices the whole time like I'm some kind of mental patient.

But I don't mind. It's exactly what I need.

The flight was terrible. I spent most of it crying and drinking little bottles of wine while my fellow passengers leaned far, far away. I tried not to think about Marc or the fact that I blew my one opportunity to make a difference and follow my dreams.

My camera is in my purse, the one thing that might bring me comfort besides the numbing of the alcohol, but

I can't even bring myself to pull it out. It has all the pictures from my weekend with Marc and the thought makes me want to cry all over again.

When we get home, Mom is waiting with my favorite old sweats and one of Dad's T-shirts. I change and she feeds me empanadas and then I crash hard in my old room, falling asleep to the sound of my mother whispering *dulces sueños* in my ear and kissing my forehead, just like she did when I was little.

When I wake up, the sun is shining and I feel about a thousand times better. So much better that I pull out my camera, but as soon as I see the first picture of Marc on the beach, laughing, head thrown back, his eyes crinkled at the corners, the stabbing pain in my chest nearly cripples me all over again.

"Too soon," I mutter before shutting the damn thing off and putting it back in my purse.

"I think she's awake," a loud voice whispers from outside my door.

"Shut up, Gabby, you're too freaking loud."

"Oh, and that wasn't loud? Why don't you just shout at me?"

"I'm awake, guys," I call out.

A second later, the door flings open and both of my sisters jump on the bed, one on either side. They hug me like I'm the meat in their sister sandwich and then snuggle down next to me on top of the comforter.

"I missed you," Gabby says, kissing my forehead.

"I missed you guys, too."

"I didn't say I missed your punk ass," Gemma says, but since she's snuggled up to my other side, I don't really believe her. "Are you ready to spill it? Everything this time and none of that bullshit you told me about dating Brent that was obviously a lie."

I take a deep breath. "Yeah. I'm ready."

And then I tell them all of it, from the night with Scarlett, to the photo shoot where I first met Brent and Marc, to Starlee's phone call and offer to help with my career, to the time I spent with Marc and how beautiful he is and how he helps everyone and everything around him to his own detriment. I tell them about Thanksgiving and the ride home.

I tell them about how it grew into something intense and our one blissful weekend—leaving out some of the sexy details, but they get the drift.

Then I tell them about what happened when the article hit, and how I discovered Brent apparently was falling for me and everything that was said before I totally lost my shit.

"Marc wasn't using you as a means to an end. He's not Lucky," Gemma says when I run out of words. "It sounds like maybe he was just talking in the heat of the moment."

"I know. But . . . I can't come between them like that. They're very close. They only have each other since their mom died and their dad is a real piece of work."

"What are you going to do now? Are you going to move home?"

"And give up everything I've been working for? Everything I crawled out of a hole to get back? No. I'm going to go back to New York and start over. Again. Or try to. Except now that I'm the focus of a celebrity sex scandal, it's going to be even harder to get people to take me seriously. How can I fight this?"

Gabby rubs my arm. "You know we'll help however we can."

"I just need a little bit of time to recover. And maybe a whole tray of Mom's chile rellenos."

Gemma laughs. "We can make that happen. And there's always a distraction available around here. We're having a little get-together at the Londons' tonight. You should come."

"They're having another party? What for this time?" Gabby asks.

"Sam's parents are out of town, so his sister Lucy is housesitting. They're having a girls' night or something."

I shrug. "If it will distract me from my train wreck of a life, I'm in."

Chapter Twenty-Two

The world can only be grasped by action, not by contemplation. The hand is the cutting edge of the mind.
        –Diane Arbus

Marc

There have been many moments in my life when I've thought, things can't possibly get any worse.

When Dad went MIA and suddenly I was a brother and a parent. When I crashed into a tree and ruined my face and any future I might have had in snowboarding. When girlfriend after girlfriend used me to get to Brent and I thought I would never meet anyone that would really see me.

When I saw the article about Gwen and me in *Stylz*. "Beauty and the Beast." How apt.

But nothing other than my own mother's death can compare to the moment that Brent accused me, rightfully so, of breaking the bro code. And then Gwen, the only person I've felt so connected to I can hardly breathe without her, disappeared out the door.

I didn't do anything to stop her.

And now I can't find her.

"Charlie, I need your help." I call her on my way to the office.

"Still not a shrink."

"Gwen's missing."

"Missing? Did you file a police report?"

"So maybe she's not missing per se. There's a distinct possibility she's avoiding me."

"What did you do?"

"Will you please meet me in my office in ten minutes?"

She sighs and grumbles something about annoying men and this is why she's a lesbian, but she agrees.

I try calling Brent again and it rings once, then goes to voicemail. Gwen's not the only one ignoring my calls.

I haven't seen him since he left the apartment yesterday. We were so busy ripping into each other we didn't even notice when Gwen left.

We said things we shouldn't have. Well, I did. I might have yelled something about how I take care of everything for him and when is he going to grow up and be a real man. For some reason, that made him leave and then ignore all my calls.

Once my head stopped pounding, I tried calling Gwen, but her phone went straight to voicemail. I went over to her apartment and she wasn't there. Her neighbor Martha hadn't seen her since that morning.

Every call I've made since then has been the same. No ringing, straight to voicemail. I tried texting, too, but no response.

I didn't sleep, too busy worrying. If something had happened, I would know, right? She was upset, she just needed space.

By the time I get to my office, Charlie is there.

"I need you to help me find her."

"How?"

I run my hands through my hair. I'm going to be bald soon. "I don't know. Hack her phone records. Hack some flight records. Start calling hospitals."

"Calm down. What happened?"

Haltingly, I tell her the whole story. Well, most of the whole story. I'm not telling her about the amazing sex.

"You love her," Charlie says once I've finished.

I blink. "Yeah. I do."

"You're an idiot."

"Yeah. I am."

She sighs. "Let me see what I can find. I'll let you know."

She leaves and I'm left alone. Once again, I call Brent. This time it rings about five times before going to voicemail.

Progress?

Maybe.

Gwen's phone is the same. Straight to voicemail.

I've never felt so frustrated and powerless in my whole life. I can't focus on anything in front of me. Instead of working on reports that are due yesterday, I start searching the web, social media sites, anywhere and everywhere looking for any mention of Gwen.

Most of the stuff that comes up is nothing new, just rehashing of the article about us being together, along with terrible photos that highlight how beautiful she is and how horrible my scars are.

I grimace at my own face.

It doesn't get better when I get a call from Dad's office.

"Marc, get in here. I need you." Then he hangs up.

For the first time in . . . ever, I don't jump to his demands. I put the phone back in the base and decide that I'm not going to listen to him. Not anymore.

Instead, I keep looking online for any Gwen sightings.

It takes Dad all of fifteen minutes to come barging into my office, red-faced and panting. "What are you doing?" he barks.

I stay seated behind my desk and lift my eyes once to take in his frustration—which gives me an inordinate amount of glee. I feel like the Grinch on Christmas after he's taken all the presents from all the Whos in Whoville and he's imagining their despair . . . before all the singing and happiness, you know. I return my gaze to the screen in front of me.

"I'm working, Dad."

"I called you. I need you."

"What do you need?" I keep clicking and tapping, not bothering to look up.

"What is wrong with you?" he bellows.

Charlie sneaks in behind his back, staying as far away from him as possible as she squeezes through the door.

"Did you find her?" I ask.

"Who are you?" Dad asks her.

"No, but I found Brent." Her eyes flick from mine to Dad's and then back, her expression serious. "He's in the hospital."

~*~

The next twenty minutes are a blur of activity. Charlie didn't have any details about what exactly happened or Brent's current condition, just that it hadn't hit the media yet because there's police involvement.

211

Dad and I rush as fast as we can down to the front of the building and get in a company car. Then we're immediately stuck in traffic.

We're in the back seat together. I'm about to explode with frustration at the amount of time it's taking to get through the city when Dad turns to me.

"Why didn't you come to my office when I called?" At least he's calm. It's weird, it's like as soon as Charlie told us about Brent, he morphed into a different person. Like her words were some kind of incantation. All of a sudden, he's serene and rational. The exact opposite of who he normally is.

"You really want to do this now?"

"It's a simple question."

"Dad." I expel a breath and run my hands through my hair. It's funny how when you've lost everything that matters, making decisions becomes so easy. "I quit."

I keep my eyes focused out the window at the people walking along the sidewalk and brace myself, waiting for an explosion.

It doesn't come.

When people have a heart attack, they do more than just sit there staring, right?

"Dad?"

"You can't quit."

I blink. He's not yelling. That's weird. "I don't like my job."

"Nobody likes their job, that's why it's called work."

"You can't make me stay. I'm a grown man, and I have no ownership interest in the company. I'm only an employee, and I'm your son. I want to be happy. I'm sorry, I really am, but I just can't do it anymore."

His face is blank. I can't read him. This can't be good.

He turns to look out the window.

So he's going to freeze me out? Is that his game plan?

"I'll find a replacement. A good one, but you can't treat them badly. Please."

Still, he says nothing and we continue the drive in deafening silence.

When we're a few blocks from the hospital, we hop out of the car and run.

We find Brent in the ER. He's okay. He's been grazed by a bullet in the left shoulder.

"What the hell happened?" I ask, right after I hug him and squeeze his face in my hands like I used to do when we were young and he suffered a bad tackle, to make sure he's really here and really alive. He's sitting on a hospital bed, in his jeans and a T-shirt. There's gauze wrapped around his left bicep.

Dad doesn't say anything. He stands on the other side of the hospital bed, listening.

"Marissa," Brent says.

"Marissa *shot* you?"

Brent nods. "Marissa is the chicken stalker."

"Chicken stalker?" Dad asks.

"I'll explain later," I tell him. "How did you find out?"

"Well, I'm still pissed at you, by the way, but I also love you because you're my brother and I was even more pissed at Marissa for running that damn article. We all know it's her behind these stories. I had my attorney file a defamation suit against her, and when she found out, she showed up at the apartment door. I was trying to get her to leave but then our neighbors came out to see the ruckus. She dropped her purse while she was flailing her arms around and hitting me, and out came a chicken picture."

"A chicken picture?" I ask.

"What the hell?" Dad says.

"Yep. Along with a few sheets of the weird vellum paper my stalker has been mailing me. I called her on it and told her I was going to have a restraining order issued, and she lost her mind. It was like a bad soap opera. It was all, *if I can't have you, no one can*, and when I told her how unoriginal that was and asked if she could come up with something less derivative, she pulled out a gun and shot me, then ran."

"Holy shit."

"Yeah. Thankfully, she's a terrible shot. One of the neighbors had already called security, and they got her almost immediately."

"You could have been killed."

"But I wasn't. And I'm going to have a badass scar that's way cooler than yours. And a better story."

I laugh, relieved. "That's true."

"I'm glad you're okay, Son," Dad says.

"Thanks for coming here, guys. I know how busy you are."

"I'm not going to be busy anymore. I quit."

Brent smiles. "Good."

Dad clears his throat. "I'm glad you're okay, Brent. I think you guys have more things to discuss. I'm going back to the office."

So much for showing emotions or sympathy for his son being in the hospital.

He's clearly not happy about what I told him, but what can I do about it? I can't let his problems become mine. Not anymore. And I'm actually surprised he didn't totally freak out on me. The calm gangster routine is new and a little scary.

But I can't worry about him now.

Once he's gone, it's just me and Brent.

"So you don't totally hate me anymore?" I ask.

He releases a sigh and his shoulders slump a little. "I never hated you. How could I? And I've been thinking about the things you said. You weren't entirely wrong with the ego comments. And I do rely on you too much. It's time for me to stand on my own and deal with things that I've been putting off."

Before I can ask what those things are, he continues. "It's just that ever since Bella broke up with me, and then all this stuff with Gwen . . . I've felt, I don't know, insecure. It's not a comfortable feeling."

"Tell me about it."

"Why didn't you tell me what was going on with you and Gwen?"

I pull at the collar of my shirt, loosening my tie. "I don't know. I didn't think she wanted me like I wanted her. It was a nonissue. But then it wasn't and I got wrapped up in the idea of having her. She's everything I didn't know I needed. And I think she really wanted me, too."

"She's a smart girl."

I shrug. "I don't think it matters anymore."

"Why not?"

"She's gone off the grid. I can't find her. I've been to her apartment, I've had Charlie hacking computer systems . . ."

"She's close with her family. Do you think she would have gone home?"

The lightbulb goes on. "Why didn't I think of that?" I can only blame the stress and lack of sleep. I fumble for my phone, pulling it out of my pocket.

There's a missed call from Charlie.

She answers after one ring.

"What did you find?"

"She left on a flight to Reno yesterday at five."

"You're a goddess."

215

"I know."

We hang up and I look at Brent. "You were right. She's there."

"Do you love her?"

"Yes."

"Then go get her."

I swallow. "Do you think it will be that easy?"

"Probably not, but I've thought of a way maybe I can help smooth the way."

Chapter Twenty-Three

The truth is the best picture, the best propaganda.
    –Robert Capa

Gwen

"*Mija*, you need to eat more."

"Mom, I just ate three helpings of ceviche."

"You are too skinny. Here. Have some rice pudding."

"Mom! Okay, fine."

I can never say no to rice pudding. Or flan. She knows my weakness, this person who birthed me.

She leaves me in the living room in front of the TV, wrapped in blankets like it's outer Siberia, a bowl of rice pudding in my hands and a heart full of doubt.

I'm sure I overreacted, leaving New York like I did. But I'm going back. I have to talk to Marc. And Brent. I have to find a way to fix . . . everything. It's all my fault. But I'm not quite ready to face reality yet.

I'm glad I'm here. This is a way better place to watch *Bridget Jones's Diary* and listen to Taylor Swift while I cry into massive amounts of food. I definitely won't starve.

The front door opens and then Gemma's voice. "Gwen! Where are you? You're supposed to be over at the Londons'." A few seconds later, she finds me in my blanket fort.

"Have you even showered?"

I point my spoon at her. "Don't judge me."

"They're waiting for us next door."

"Good for them."

"Stop being a child. You said you would come over."

"I guess I did."

"They really want to meet you. And it's very casual, think yoga pants and sleepwear. You don't even have to change."

"Can I bring my blankets?"

"Ugh. Fine. Maybe it will help cover your stank."

I put on my slippers and we tromp across the side yard and over to the neighbors.

Gemma knocks at the front door and it swings open a few seconds later.

"You found her." Lucy, Sam's sister, answers the door. She's a few years younger than me, but I've always found her a little intimidating. She's nice enough, it's just that when she was sixteen she was working on her PhD and when I was sixteen I was smoking weed and watching *Evil Dead* movies.

"It's so nice to see you again, Gwen," Lucy says, stepping back and motioning for us to enter.

"It's nice to see you, too. Thanks for inviting me."

"Everyone is in the living room. I'm making popcorn and getting the drinks ready. Sam and Jensen are upstairs watching the game and they promised not to interfere."

"I'll help you," Gemma says.

She's going to leave me with strangers?

Close. She hustles me into the living room and yells, "Everyone, this is my sister, Gwen. Don't freak her out," and then hustles right out.

The three people in the living room, two women in recliners and a guy on the couch, all turn and gape at me. I thought this was a girls' night?

"Hi," I say from inside my blanket cocoon. "My sister misspoke since obviously I'm the one who's not supposed to freak you out."

"Come sit with me," the guy says, patting the open seat on the couch next to him. "We're discussing the merits of sleeping with someone on the first date and we need another opinion."

Okay, girls' night makes sense again. He's gay. Thank God.

"I'm Ted." My new friend pats me on the shoulder when I sit down. Probably since he can't shake my hands, which are clutching my blankets to me like they'll protect me from the world.

"There is no merit to giving up the goods on a first date," one of the girls speaks. She's petite with light brown hair.

Ted leans over and whispers, "That's Freya. Her stance is to be a prude for as long as you can."

"Um, clearly if you want to get laid, there's merit."

"That's Bethany." He points at the girl with curly blonde hair. "She's a tramp."

"I can hear you, Ted. And might I remind you that before you became all old and complacent you were more of a tramp than I could ever be."

He ignores her and asks me, "Would you like to weigh in?"

I shrug. "Do whatever makes you happy because you never know how long it's going to last."

"Thank you," Bethany says.

"That wasn't necessarily an agreement to your argument and why are we having this conversation?" I ask.

Ted shrugs. "Bethany can't keep a man."

A carrot flies through the air and hits him on the arm.

"I'm the only single person left and it sucks," Bethany explains. "Everyone is all married or coupled up, and I can't even get past a first date."

Freya snorts. "Well maybe if you stopped screwing them on the first date . . ."

"You know, I don't always screw them. Some of them we just sleep. Or you know, other things, but regardless, it shouldn't matter what I'm doing or not doing. Why bother waiting? That's the fun part. And it's the easiest way to know if you're compatible with someone."

Lucy and Gemma come into the room, their arms loaded with soda and popcorn and snacks.

Freya continues the argument while grabbing a soda from Lucy. "Compatibility is about more than sleeping with someone. Lucy, back me up."

"Actually, determining whether coitus will be satisfactory is a legitimate concern."

Freya groans. "Lucy! For God's sake would you quit referring to it as coitus?"

"What else would I call it?"

"Sex?"

"The word sex is derived from the Latin word *sexus*, which refers to males and females collectively, whereas coitus describes the action of sexual union."

There's silence for a few long seconds.

Then Freya speaks. "I don't know how to respond to that."

"Are we going to watch a movie?" Gemma asks.

There's a bit of shuffling as someone puts the movie in, and people grab snacks and drinks and Ted hands me a bag of M&M's.

Apparently we're screening nineties chick flicks, because the opening credits to *Clueless* come up on the flat screen. But the general silence doesn't last long. Cher is lamenting the reasons she doesn't date high school boys and the chatter and debate in the room around me ignites again.

I listen, enjoying the banter, until the focus turns on me.

"So, Gwen, what brought you back into town?" Freya asks.

Bethany elbows her in the side.

"Nothing important," I say.

Shared glances dance around the room.

Dammit. They know.

"You can tell us," Ted says, patting my head.

"We need for you to give us the dirt. We have no drama," Freya adds. "We need someone to live through vicariously. We're all in serious committed relationships."

"Not all of us," Bethany says.

"You don't count, trollop."

"Hey!"

"Well it's your own fault you're alone. You make terrible choices."

"She's not wrong," says Ted.

Lucy interjects. "Bethany's choices are not terrible. We all have to learn from our past mistakes. It's how we grow."

"Pft, so you say." Freya rolls her eyes.

Lucy shakes her head. "I don't say, I know. We discussed it at length the other day. She's going to focus on her career and working through the inner turmoil sustained from her upbringing."

"Oh here we go with the Freud bullshit."

"Freud is not bullshit."

Freya snorts out a laugh. "You're so funny when you curse. You sound like a prissy school marm trying to be tough. Anyway, Gwen, tell us about this hot football player guy and don't leave anything out. We want to hear all the details, including what his junk looks like."

"I never saw his junk."

"Boring," Ted intones.

"I saw his brother's junk."

"Slightly better," Ted says. "Spill it."

I sigh and consider it. Why not?

I go through the whole story. Again. When I'm done, the entire room is watching me with wide eyes.

Bethany is the first to speak. "So, what you're telling us is that Brent Crawford, *the* Brent Crawford, the guy on the TV with the tight pants and the hot face and the bajillions of dollars, he wanted you, and you ran away?"

Ted answers for me. "Were you even listening? It's not really about Brent, it's about Marc, his brother."

"She loves Marc," Gemma interjects.

"This is really a problem we have to solve?" Freya asks. "Oh, no, two men love me and they're both gorgeous and successful. My wallet's too small for my fifties, and my diamond shoes are too tight!"

"You totally stole that from Chandler Bing," Bethany says.

"Um, excuse me, that's Ms. Chanandler Bong, to you, slut-face."

Their bickering is interrupted when someone upstairs starts yelling.

"What is that?" Lucy presses mute on the remote and then we can hear it.

"Gemma," Sam hollers from somewhere upstairs, "put on channel four!"

"What? Why?" She calls back.

"Just do it!"

She looks at Lucy, who shrugs and clicks the remote a few times.

There's some stomping going on upstairs and I barely notice Sam and Jensen entering the room behind us because Brent is on the TV.

He's standing in front of a crowd, dressed in a T-shirt and jeans. There's a bunch of press in front of him, all lined up with microphones and cameras. White flashes snap on his face as he speaks.

"Turn it up," Sam says.

Lucy pushes a button and the volume comes up.

". . . so Marissa Reeves attempted to kill you?"

"Holy shit," I breathe, dropping my security blankets on the couch and moving closer to the TV.

"That's correct. She received some correspondence from my lawyer and didn't take it well. She came to my apartment and she had a gun. Luckily, it was only a graze and on my left arm." He lifts the sleeve of his shirt to show his arm, which is indeed wrapped in white gauze. *"Marissa is now facing multiple charges of harassment, stalking, attempted murder, and illegally firing a weapon within city limits, but that's not why I'm here today. She hurt people that I love with her false allegations and I want to set the record straight."*

He takes a breath.

"Oh my God he's going to tell the world he loves you!" Freya shoves popcorn in her mouth. "This is the best girls' night ever."

"What Marissa said about me, that I harassed and attacked her, was a lie. I knew no one would believe me if I just denied it, and that's when my agent decided it would be best for me to be in a relationship. A fake relationship, with Gwen McDougall."

There's a swell of voices, and questions are thrown at him, but he raises his hands. *"Please, let me finish. None of it really matters. It was a bad decision from my agent and from me. I'm looking for a new agent now, so if any of you know anyone . . ."* The assembled crowd shuffles and laughs obligingly. *"In the end, Gwen was the one who got*

223

hurt all because she tried to help me and in the meantime fell in love with my brother. None of this is her fault and she shouldn't suffer for it. She's a great photographer, and she'll make a great sister-in-law someday."

Gemma hits me in the arm. "Are you getting married?"

"What? No!"

Then Brent looks straight into the camera. *"Gwen, if you're watching this, Marc has been trying to reach you. Will you please turn on your phone and take his call?"*

The entire living room turns to gape at me.

I'm as stunned as they are.

"Where the hell is your phone?" Gemma asks.

"I . . . shit, it's in my purse. I had to turn it off when I was on the plane and I never turned it back on."

The doorbell rings.

Everyone freezes. We're all looking at each other, dumbfounded, and then in a burst of motion, we all race for the front door.

Sam makes it there first and swings it open, everyone crowded behind him trying to see. I, of course, end up in the back behind Ted and Jensen and I can't see anything.

"Who is it?" I ask.

"Is Gwen here?"

My heart stops in my chest and then restarts in double time.

I would know that voice anywhere.

It's Marc.

He's here?

"Yeah, man, come on in." He steps back and runs into Gemma. "Jesus, you guys are ridiculous. Would you back up and let a guy in?"

They all part right down the middle and I have the insane urge to laugh.

It's like a movie.

A really weird movie with the most absurd people who couldn't possibly exist in real life, but the thought is short-lived because he's *here*.

He came.

He flew all the way across the country because my phone was off.

Our eyes meet and everyone else fades into the background. He looks terrible. Exhausted. A bit grey around the eyes and he obviously hasn't shaved in a couple of days, but there's a sheen of hope on his face.

His gaze flicks to our audience and then back to me. "Gwen, I'm so sorry about what I said. You were right about everything. I'm the biggest moron in the world for letting you walk out my door without stopping you. I have no excuse but I love you so much. Please, come home with me?"

There's a collective sigh from the peanut gallery.

"Nice apology, dude." Sam holds up his hand for a high five.

Gemma grabs his wrist and pulls it down. "Shhhhhh! You're ruining their moment."

I bite my lip to stop myself from laughing and turn toward the crowd. "Will you guys give us a minute?"

There are nods and yeah sures and they start filtering back into the main part of the house.

"You're not getting married, right?" Bethany whispers as she passes me.

"Stop being so bitter about everyone having a relationship but you," Freya says. "It's your own fault."

Ted groans. "Not this again."

They disappear back to the living room, and when we're finally alone I turn back to Marc.

"Do you think that any part of you wants me purely because of Brent? Because you want to outdo him or salve your own insecurities?"

His mouth pops open. "What? No. Absolutely not."

"You said you love me . . ."

"I do."

"What do you love about me then?"

There's no hesitation. "I love the way you treat people. Like they're important. You treat everyone the same, no matter who they are. Whether it's a famous footballer and his scarred brother, or some guys from Jersey at a football game." He takes a step toward me. "I love the way you aren't afraid to be yourself, and you never let adversity stop you from chasing your dreams." He takes another step. "I love the way you dance when you're happy, like you don't care who's watching, and I love how you shimmy a little when you eat really good food." He chuckles and takes one last step. There's only a thin strip of air between us. "Mostly, I love how you make me feel unafraid to take chances. Knowing that you believe in me makes me believe it, too."

My heart is almost too full to speak.

"Do you believe me?" He takes both of my hands in his, searching my eyes.

"I do." I take a deep breath. "And I love you, too."

The tension falls away from his body. "Thank God." And then his arms are around me, he's grabbing me up, and we're hugging and he peppers my face with kisses.

There's cheering and catcalls from somewhere down the hall.

I wipe away happy tears and laugh and Marc kisses me again. A real, long, satisfying kiss that makes me want to rip off my clothes and do him against the wall right now.

"They're very interesting." He pulls back for a second to speak.

"That's putting it mildly."

He pulls back a little further and grabs my hands. "So I quit my job."

"You did?"

"And I talked to Starlee and you have another shot at your presentation if you can make it back to New York next week."

"I do?"

He kisses my fingertips. "And if you get it, which I believe you will because you're talented and amazing, you might benefit from having an assistant."

I see where he is going with this, but I play along. "I might?"

"And since I'm looking for a new job, I was thinking maybe I could apply?"

"You've got it all figured out, don't you?"

His smile is everything. "I do."

"There's only one thing I have to ask."

"What's that?"

"Are there any stipulations about boning my assistant?"

He laughs. "Nope. No stipulations at all. Boning is encouraged in my contract."

And then we're laughing together, in between kisses. His lips pepper over my face.

In between laughs I manage to say, "That sounds perfect."

Epilogue

Life rarely presents fully finished photographs.
An image evolves, often from a single strand of
visual interest — a distant horizon, a moment
of light, a held expression.
                                        –Sam Abell

Marc

Gwen stands in the center of the empty living room. Her arms are crossed over her chest and her back is to me as she gazes out the small window.

"The truck is packed up and ready to go."

She turns and smiles. "Okay." Then she resumes her stance. Her eyes are tired.

We're both sweaty and dirty from moving all day. Her face is free of makeup and she's wearing old jeans that have a hole in the knee.

She's still the most beautiful person I've ever seen in my life.

I wrap my arms around her from behind, propping my head on her shoulder. "Are you all right? Regretting your decision yet?"

She chuckles and relaxes back against me. "Nope. You can't get rid of me that easy. It's just weird to be leaving the one place I've lived in the city."

"You can come back and visit sometime. I'm sure Bethany won't mind." We sublet Gwen's place to one of her sister's friends since her lease isn't up for another year.

"I'm sure she won't mind me visiting but she might mind working for your father."

In a series of fortuitous events, my father's assistant Alex quit not so unexpectedly. I needed a new employee. Bethany needed a change of scenery. Now she's moving to the city and has a new job and a place to get her started. Plus she'll be checking our mail and watering our plants while we're gone. Smiles all around. "It will be okay. She might actually be able to handle him. Being a pretty blonde won't hurt. I tried to scare her off, but she didn't seem concerned."

We're silent for a moment, standing by the window in the remains of the day, gazing at the view. It's not much to look at, a brick building across the way and the street below where the occasional pedestrian or vehicle passes by. But I would stand here with her for hours if it made her feel better.

"Have you talked to Brent?" she asks.

"Just a text."

She rubs gentle hands down my tense arms and I try to relax. I haven't seen Brent since the morning in the hospital. By the time Gwen and I came back to New York a week later, he had left.

It's been two months. At first, he had the excuse of playoffs and team stuff, but now he's finished out the season and I have yet to see him. All I've gotten is a few random texts to let me know he's okay. If it wasn't for the occasional paparazzi shot and his meager attempts at contact, I might have thought he was dead. He must be staying in hotels or with other friends.

"He'll come around," Gwen says.

"I hope so. I would like to see him before we leave the country."

We're flying out in less than a month. Gwen's proposal to Warren at *News Weekly* went amazingly well. They gave her the green light within a week. We were a little surprised — not that they would want to run her idea, she's brilliant and amazing — but since Brent fired Starlee, we weren't sure if that would affect her chances. Apparently not.

We stand there for a few more minutes in comfortable silence, gazing out at nothing but content all the same. Mostly content. There's something going on with Brent, more than the Gwen stuff. Something he hasn't been sharing. It's not like him to keep things from me, but I can't force him. I can just hope he'll let me in, eventually.

"Are you ready to go home?" I ask finally.

We have to drop off most of her belongings in storage. We're only taking the essentials back to my place. Our place. We've basically been living in each other's pockets anyway for the last two months, so it's not a huge change, but it feels important, meshing our earthly possessions together.

She turns in my arms. "You're my home."

I gasp. "That was so cheesy."

She grins. "Yes! I win the cheeseball award today."

"You do not. I had that line earlier, about how you mean more to me than the entire sun and universe and galaxy, remember?"

"That was so not as good as my home comment."

"Puh-lease." I totally win.

"I think I can change your mind." She unzips my pants and reaches inside.

I suck a breath in between my teeth. "I'm listening."

"We never did it in the kitchen." Her grasp is firm and she strokes me once. Twice.

What were we talking about? I pick her up, jarring her hand out of my jeans and lifting her by the ass. Her legs straddle me, her arms looping around my neck, her lips close enough to taste.

Oh right, the kitchen. "That's because one full-grown person can't fit in here, let alone two."

"I disagree."

"Let's test that theory, shall we?" I walk with her still wrapped around me the couple of paces it takes to get to the microscopic kitchen. I set her on the counter and glance around. "I guess we do fit."

She kisses me then, her hands sliding against my scalp, sending goose bumps down my arms, and then she speaks against my mouth. "We fit perfectly."

The End

Are you ready for Brent's story?

Check out my website to get updates! Expected release 11/2018!

www.authormaryframe.com

About the Author

Go here to sign up for the newsletter!
www.authormaryframe.com

Mary Frame is a full-time mother and wife with a full-time job. She has no idea how she manages to write novels except that it involves copious amounts of wine. She doesn't enjoy writing about herself in third person, but she does enjoy reading, writing, dancing, and damaging the eardrums of her coworkers when she randomly decides to sing to them.

She lives in Reno, Nevada, with her husband, two children, and a border collie named Stella.

She LOVES hearing from readers and will not only respond but likely begin stalking them while tossing out hearts and flowers and rainbows! If that doesn't creep you out, email her at: maryframeauthor@gmail.com
Follow her on Twitter: @marewulf
Like her Facebook author page:
www.facebook.com/AuthorMaryFrame
Imperfect Series — All books are stand-alone and can be read in any order! With a guaranteed HEA!
Book One: Imperfect Chemistry
Book Two: Imperfectly Criminal
Book Three: Practically Imperfect
Book Four: Picture Imperfect
Extraordinary Series — Not stand-alone novels! Must be read in order!
Book One: Anything But Extraordinary
Book Two: A Life Less Extraordinary
Book Three: Extraordinary World

95018565R00144

Made in the USA
Middletown, DE
23 October 2018